SAY HER NAME

A SID RUBIN SILICON ALLEY ADVENTURE

STEFANI DEOUL

Bywater
BOOKS

Ann Arbor
2019

Bywater Books

Copyright © 2019 Stefani Deoul

All rights reserved. No part of this book may be
reproduced, stored in a retrieval system, or transmitted
in any form or by any means, without prior permission
in writing from the publisher.

Print ISBN: 978-1-61294-161-5

Bywater Books First Edition: December 2019

Printed in the United States of America on acid-free paper.

Cover designer: Ann McMan, TreeHouse Studio

Bywater Books
PO Box 3671
Ann Arbor MI 48106-3671
www.bywaterbooks.com

Quotes on page 155: Wiesel, Elie. *Night*.
New York City: Hill & Wang, 1960.

To: 14

Love: 16

"People are trapped in history
and history is trapped in them."

—James Baldwin, "Stranger in the Village"

PROLOGUE

I am ducking, dodging, shooting, and . . . and . . . and yes, scoring! It's a direct hit! I watch as shrapnel of snowflakes run down my opponent's face, leaving telltale trails on his cheeks, and clinging beads on the edge of his woolen hat. My head swells, my chest puffs . . .

. . . and welcome to Central Park, somewhere between the North Meadow and The Loch, blanketed by multiple feet of snow still coming down, and thousands of kids still pouring in. It is I think every child's fantasy come to life. We are snow-day'd off from school, having a free-for-all, blizzard-induced snowball fight of the century.

Ça envoie du pâté! It is pretty freaking awesome! There have to be hundreds of kids here already, and more keep pouring into the park from every direction.

It's sort of like Ned Stark woke up, looked out, and proclaimed, "winter is coming," and from everywhere in the city White Walkers are stampeding, and the park is the wall, and we, we are the sea of hooded, hatted, masked, scarfed, gloved, ducking, weaving, bobbing, bumping, drift impaling, packing, loading, and throwing Night's Watch, here to save Manhattan from those who would do her harm.

Okay, maybe that's not exactly apt.

Maybe, perhaps, I am indulging in just the teensiest bit of hyperbole.

Because, in truth, given our movements are somewhat constrained by our goose down vs. synthetic down layers,

1

we are more like "winter is coming, the parody," in which an open air arena is filled with hordes of drunken, reeling snowmen rather than any kind of lean, mean fighting machines, and those white, packed fluff bombs tossed at each other are way more likely to hit the person located three people over, rather than their intended target.

Whatever.

Because despite *our* layers of pants and assorted puffy-synthetic challenges, we, the spectacular septuplet—a.k.a. Jimmy-Imani-Ari-Vikram-Joe-Ava-and me, Sid "do-not-call-me-Sidonie" Rubin a.k.a. our side of the maybe sixty or seventy kids within our bombing radius—are killing it.

Septuplet? Not fierce five? Ava? Joe? Aha! As always, I thank you my friends for being right here with me, but unfortunately—*shifting right!*—now is not a good time to stop and explain. I do promise to get back to you right after I bend, pack, and fire.

Which may take another minute or two. Because, before I can squat to scoop more snow, a movement to my left intrudes upon the edge of my vision, and I somehow manage to flex back and stay on my feet, all while pirouetting about three inches in a left-leaning spin, in time to clear for Jimmy's unleashed perfect spiral.

And go.

Dropping down, I quickly pack snow into a shape close enough to being a ball if no one scrutinizes it too closely. Rearmed I rise, moving my arm so it is positioned to throw. I deke. I feint. I fake. And then I make my fatal mistake. I spare one moment to steal a look at Ava. And wham! I freeze.

Ava caught my little side-eye glance, and in response a coy, come hither grin begins curving as she crosses her wrists, her gloved hands bobbing with her fingers formed in the letter "s" position, a move better known as the "making out" sign. And that, that is all it takes.

In spite of the cold and my soaking wet gloves, my down-encased body is now a kiln with an inferno blazing

2

inside. Hot enough to melt, well, I suppose ice. But really anything. Especially me.

Only I don't melt. I just stand here with my boot-encased feet rooted to my spot, snowball melting in palm, until a wet-incoming scores a direct hit. To my face.

Did you know the Swedes have more than ninety-five ways to describe the act of rubbing snow in one's face?

Before I can fully wrap my brain around this tidbit of awesomeness, not to mention suck the once-again-loosening mucus membranes back into my nose, Jimmy's right arm thrusts me out of the path of another incoming, launching me backward, right into Ari, who stumbles into Imani, who then goes flying, tumbling down the slope and into the ravine.

Ava, the only one of us who can actually see our version of the Three Stooges unfold, is laughing, which, were it anyone else would have pissed me off no end, but instead has me enthralled from my derriere-on-the-ground point of view. Which leaves Jimmy turning to see what is so funny. And that, that, my friends, is when we hear the scream.

It's Imani. Only this isn't an "I'm tumbling down, save me" scream. Oh no. This scream does not match that tumble.

For just a millisecond, all other sound drops out. Jimmy looks at me and I look at him and as random as it sounds, my first—and only—thought is, uh-oh, here we go again.

I don't know why I think that. I also don't know how I know this scream is different from all others, but I know it is. And so does Jimmy.

I scramble back to my feet, racing down one step behind him. And for just a second I glance back and see Vikram and Joe giving chase.

But not Ava.

Ava is standing there, perched at the top of the slope, looking down at me. Only this time, instead of her look turning me hot with lust, it sends a chill down my spine. But I have no time to stop and sort it out. Imani needs me. And I am already running two steps behind.

ONE

But not Ava. That thought echoes through my mind as I slip and slide my way down the slope. Which might make this a most opportune time to, as promised, bring you up to speed.

It all began with my hunt for my Mystery Dream Girl, a.k.a. my MDG.

And I promise, I shall try for succinctness and key points. But considering who am I, I make no guarantees.

To begin, let us travel back in time until a vision appears. There we are, the fearless five, trapped in the soul-sucking, cinderblock, spirit-bannered, fluorescently lit school cafeteria, suffering from serious latte withdrawal and thus incredibly weakened, vulnerable, and exposed to some kind of undefined attack, when exactly that happens.

Only it is not an attack on the fearless five, but an attack from within. It is our very own Vikram Patel who pushes, pulls, and finally ropes us into participating in the school's annual robotics competition.

And I could bore you with many details, but instead, I will simply give props to Vik for having a plan that worked. We were sprung from our parental detention, which had led us to our near-catastrophic lunchroom fate, a dire situation brought on by our so-called previous so-called shenanigans.

So, despite some unattractive kicking and screaming—hey, I'm owning it—our participation garnered us rehabilitated status, and we are once again upstanding citizens, and newly sanctioned members of the school robotics team, the Cooper Thoriums. Where we find ourselves invested in surprising, but not really surprising if you think about it, ways.

Talking star quarterback Jimmy "Five Fingers" Flynn into handling the driving of the bots, a position requiring one possessed of most excellent hand-eye coordination, was kind of like a no-brainer. Imani "all the world's a stage" Cruz becoming Chief of Construction? Seems way out there until you put it together with all her stage experience. Me? Coding? Big yawn.

But Ari "always larger-than-life" Wilson, leaving boyfriend/coach Vikram Patel to work the business plan side with co-head coach, the impossibly charming, super-chill Marcus Johnston? Now that, my friends, that was an eyebrow raising, savacious move. Savacious because it is both glorious and savage, and genius on so many levels—from the simple, obvious "great for the college application" to the complex layers, designed to remind Vik that she's her own woman, not to be taken for granted. Savacious.

Okay. I hear you. But you know, savaciousness does deserve a moment. And . . . speeding up . . . getting on with the getting on . . .

. . . and go. We immersed ourselves in a massively multi-player online role-playing game a.k.a. an MMORPG called *Contagion*, where we went hunting to trap a trophy thief. We joined forces for a life and death chase through virtual time and place. We came, we saw, we conquered, and no stopping us now, we continued our worldlier conquest at the robotic competition, where, right as we are conquering, it happened.

I looked up and there she was. Right there.

And there I was, gobsmacked.

The rest of my day is a blur. As Thoriums, we did okay. We did not—sadly—win our twentieth anniversary competition, but we did "level up" enough to finish in second place, which I categorize as a miracle given that my mind still remains a bit of a blank.

I know there were awards and scholarships, but my eyes were continuously scanning the crowds, desperately trying to surreptitiously catch one more glimpse of her, but to no avail.

Instead, I kept replaying the scene, *our* scene, almost in slow motion. I see myself see her, her dark hair and pale green eyes, her hands flying about. I watch myself as I approach, introducing myself, risking everything to ask her if she'd like to get something to eat later on.

She stops briefly as I approach, then her hands begin flying again, and I realize they aren't just waving. I realize she is signing—but not to me.

I watch as her friend turns around. He introduces himself. His name is Joe. He doesn't introduce her to me, but delivers her message, "Come back when you can ask her directly."

The gauntlet had been thrown.

Which I, of course, pick right on up. Don't even stop to give it a first thought, never mind a second. Miraculously this starts out way better than one would think. Probably because I wasn't. Thinking that is. It was kind of like a reflex. She threw it; I picked it up.

Nearly as intoxicating as a double dog dare, a gauntlet is not to be ignored.

But occasionally it is to be put on hold. At least until after I can escape the what-seemed-like-a-good-idea-at-the-time celebratory dinner with the family, where of course my normally petulant, silent younger brother, Jean, decides to uncharacteristically live it up, rambling on all about how he helped out. Which, he did. He is occasionally useful. Tonight, however, he is not. Useful. At all.

I am convinced the concept of delayed gratification comes from someone who got caught in familial dinner hell.

Mercifully Jean shuts up and the meal ends. We do finally get home. Whereupon I immediately execute the parental kiss-kiss, wave goodnight, race to my room, boot my laptop, sink to the far side of my bed, prop my feet against the wall, interlace my fingers, stretch arms out, bring arms back, stretch neck left—no crack, right—two mini cracks, and get to work.

Step one. Identify the object of my . . . of my what, exactly? I wrack my brain. And not because I can't complete the sentence, I can. But because I'm not sure I want to. When I hear it in my head, it's cringe inducing, and yet. Big deep breath. Let it out.

She is the object of my heart's desire.

Eye roll. Big eye roll. Double circuit. Still there.

Eye rolling can't make it less accurate. Whoever she is, she is at least my brain and body's desire, if not my heart's.

All I really know is she's like some spectral being who's taken over a rather large portion of my mind's eye. I see her whipping her head around to look at me, laughing at something only we know, some private conversation only we are having, and then, just before I can lean over and touch, she disappears from view, leaving me physically aching for her.

And no, I don't need anyone to point out this was a mere seven hours ago. I am quite well aware. But seven hours is an eternity when it's driven by her off-colored pale green eyes teasing me, pulling me deeper into a pool I want to willingly dive into.

And seven hours is actually four hundred and twenty minutes. Which, when calculated that way, does add up to at least a "quite a while" if not even "a long time." Especially when teetering on a precipice.

Coup de foudre. She is a strike of lightning.

I look up through my windows and make a vow. One day I shall find you and tell you *ouand je t'ai vu pour la première fois, c'était le coup de foudre.* The first time I saw you, I fell head over heels.

Enough. I blink, shake my head, and begin to do what I do best: devise a game plan. Which brings me back to step one. Identification.

I begin scrolling through hours of video from *FIRST* Inspires Robotics Competition. It's amazing how many kids, and their parents, needed to get their participation uploaded as soon as they could. It's also amazing how many of them shoot only their children and no one else!

I am now over an hour in, meaning more than five hundred minutes have passed since she turned and walked away, and I got nothing. Well almost nothing. Some parent I don't know got a great picture of Jimmy and me, which I have swiped for my wall.

I also mobilized what I think is a surefire backup. You'd think being one of the fearsome five means lots of personalized accessible coverage. And it does. Although Ari's Mom isn't really helpful, Imani's parents and my parents are basically a bust. They've shared a couple of clips, some stills, nothing of consequence, but Jimmy's mom, Reiko, turns out to be a jackpot. Or maybe she's just, wait for it—knee-slapper alert ahead—the mother lode! Come on, don't hate me, you know that's what being giddy gets us.

Sobering up. Jimmy's mom wanted to stream some of this to her mother, who is in Japan visiting *her* mother, so she recorded everything, and then, just in case she somehow missed anything, asked Vik's parents for their three phones' worth of data!

MDG, I know you're in there, somewhere.

It took another forty minutes, but when my phone pinged, it was Jimmy, and he had it. He found it on his mother's phone, "Sending it now."

And it was even more embarrassing than I thought. You see, I thought having to ask Jimmy to send it would be the embarrassing part, but I was wrong. When I saw the footage, it turns out while Jimmy's mom was shooting him, she captured him just as he waved over to Imani to get her attention, and then he pointed. So naturally Reiko turned to follow whatever he was pointing at, and there it was, digitally captured for all eternity, the embarrassing part. Me, awkwardly, at least to my eyes, trying to make conversation with this really hot girl, then figuring out she can't actually hear me.

I am a woman with a goal. There will be no time-out for mortification.

I spot her on the video, which translates to a rapid dozen or so screenshots, and I also spot that guy Joe she was with, and wait for it, behind them, their team, with . . . enlarge, with their logo.

Bull's-eye!

School name now gotten, and heading over to the old Google-ator, cross-referencing.

While my pages load, a random thought occurs to me. Jimmy's gone bizarrely quiet here. I don't know if we're growing up somehow, or if Imani did her nose wrinkle thing and explained "probably not a good time," or, most likely, tormenting me in this moment would be way too easy, even for him.

For which I am grateful. This way I get to be holed up in my room, searching for my soon-to-be next girlfriend, without an incessantly chiming Greek chorus of friends to help.

And there, on page seventeen, she is.

And even in a school photo, on a page filled with school photos, she leaps right out. My eyes lower to read the caption.

Her name is Ava. Ava Kushnir.

Ava.

I breathe it quietly and feel it making me smile. Ava. I like the name Ava. It's a palindrome.

Which one should not confuse with a semordnilap. Palindromes spell the same word forward and backward, while semordnilaps spell completely different words forward and backward, of which my favorite is stressed-desserts, as I do believe they go hand in hand, or at least hand to mouth. I know, yuk yuk yuk. But I am also quite fond of dog and god for the same reason.

But they are semordnilaps, and we are talking palindromes, which, by the way is semordnilap spelled backward.

Note to self, breathe!

It's so perfect. Ava is Ava, *Shift*. Even backward, *Command*. She is Ava. *Four*.

And screen grab.

And, save to Desktop, Ava Folder.

TWO

"Sid," Imani 's voice floats behind me, catching me just as I'm following behind my backpack, sliding into our usual booth in what has now become our usual haunt, deep in the rear of Platitudes. "When's Ava's birthday?"

"July 28," I reply, sliding, without thinking. Then I cringe. 'Cause I know. One second too late. It's a setup.

"I hate you," I say indiscriminately to both Ari and Imani, now sliding into opposite sides of the booth and way too busy laughing and high-fiving to care. I'm not sure which one annoys me more.

"You," Ari leans forward, her newly acquired bangs sliding slightly left, "have officially become a Schmoop."

I look up, catching Ari's self-satisfied—no, that would be too high-falutin'; this is just old-school smug—look. It's simple, direct, and deliciously evil. Her smug glances past me, over to Imani, which sends me lunging for Imani's phone, located on the table conveniently between us. Again, I'm one second too late. Imani has the epitome of catlike reflexes.

And thus, with phone in hand, she stares me down, waiting. I give. She flourishes the phone and types.

"Schmoop has a c," a suddenly helpful Ari chimes back in. "It's schmoop, s-c-h-m-o-o-p. Without the c it's a website for people who want to skip the read and go straight for the study guide."

Imani squeals and I brace myself for what's coming. I might not know schmoop, but I know whatever schmoop is, they are going to think it's hilarious. And, yes, I'm correct as roughly ten seconds later Imani proceeds to read aloud, apparently for her own benefit and delight because we all know it's not for mine.

"A fanfic," dramatic pause, "with LOTS of fluff," dramatic pause, "or with a more intense level of fluff." This time the pause comes with a hand to heart and a shoulder lean in. "So fluffy, as to say it was schmoop."

She accentuates her enlightenment with a snap z formation, complete with pucker/duck face, hair toss, lean back, smirk, tight-lipped grin, concluding by throwing a knowing glance at Ari.

I give her performance a seven. A little overwrought for my taste.

"Oh my god, Ari, it's perfect. You are so totally right." Her voice is way too soprano and fake. All that's missing is a clutching of her throat. Forget seven. Her performance is rapidly sinking to a five.

"Sid, you have officially become a schmoopie. You are so busy researching and outlining your own fanfic romance, you are totally lost in real life."

Our waitress interrupts my education of schmoopification, but I know it's only a brief respite. This will be too entertaining for a simple "moving on."

And because there's no win here for me, I go big, ordering both a black & white shake and a basket of fries. Carbs and grease are a necessary counter in times such as this. It's hard to over-petulant one's self with a mouthful of fries and a shake chaser.

"And," Imani returns to the land of talking, "it's becoming treacly, maudlin, and way too sugary."

I need those fries. *Now.*

"Because if I understand this correctly, to be schmoopy is to make others wince," Imani pauses for a second. "No, too soft. To be schmoopy is to make others vomit with your cavity-inducing essays of affection."

And just as I am about to whip around and protest, Ari gets back in the game, raises her "wait one moment" finger. "But to want schmoop? Perfectly normal, don't be alarmed. We all *want* schmoop. Submit."

Submit? Submit to what exactly?

First of all, this is not fair. I mean, really, how would she know?

Maybe because you have a notebook filled with dates and trivia and quotes all about Ava. Maybe that's how.

And second of all, even if it is true, she doesn't need to be snarky about it all. Romance should be sweet.

I am not rising to this bait. Nope, not biting. I am going to sit here and focus on the slit in this gnarly, cracked, red pleather booth and pick at its threads instead. No eye contact, apparently, is no deterrent for Imani.

"You know what," rhetorical question. There's no pause to see if I want to know. "It's time for you to put on your big girl pants and go ask her out. I mean really, at this point it's worse than online dating; it's profiling. Verging on stalking. Which is not funny and definitely not cool."

And with that, while I am studiously not making eye contact, Ari sneaks around, grabs my phone, and gives Imani a nod while airdropping an address, all before I can react. Then Imani throws some cash down on the table, and the two of them pull me out the door, push me down to the subway, onto the platform, and into the car, keeping me there until we exit at the DUMBO station in Brooklyn.

Yeah. I know. I never did get my fries. Oh, that wasn't your concern? Fine.

DUMBO is an acronym for Down Under the Manhattan Bridge Overpass, and not the better-known elephant. Not that I would think you would think it was the elephant, but maybe you thought it was shaped like an ear or something. You know, we can all find ourselves flummoxed at times.

13

I remember driving through Dutch Pennsylvania when I was about ten. And they had a town called Virginville. Now that might have been a bit more of a snort-giggle than a flummox, but I was only ten.

Anyway, if you go up to the top of One World Trade Center and look across, DUMBO is the neighborhood set right in between the Brooklyn Bridge and the Manhattan Bridge, and it's really expensive and very tech-centric.

And since, of course, I already boned up on Ava's Mom and Dad, I know they are big tech guru people, so it makes perfect sense.

I haven't been to DUMBO recently, but I always love coming here in the summer. It's all cobblestone streets and converted warehouses, and when you peek down the streets, there's always amazing views of the bridge. And they have Movies with a View, where they set up this outdoor movie screen and you sit on a blanket on the grass and watch movies with the city as your backdrop, and there is also Jane's Carousel, and ice cream at Fulton Ferry Landing from a shop located in the old fireboat house. Fulton Landing is actually the site of the original ferry that ran between Manhattan and Brooklyn, starting way back in 1642.

And then we could go get chocolate at Jacques Torres or go to a show at St. Ann's Warehouse, or . . .

. . . and wowzerhole. I realize I have unwittingly switched over from "my memories" to my date night fantasy. I also realize I have stopped walking and Ari and Imani are about two feet ahead, just waiting.

And they're right, big sigh, schmoopie is me.

We persevere until I get to the front of the Water Street address I know by heart, trying to gather enough courage to push the buzzer. But my palms are sweating and my heart is beating and I'm not sure this is a good idea.

Clarifying. I do think coming here was good. After all, I didn't come voluntarily; they dragged me. Which gets me much closer than climbing the steps at the West Elm, Dumbo location, and peering down from the roof did. Hey, smitten kitten. You do know.

But now that I'm here, fantastic, I can leave knowing my way right to the door. So, I can come back another day and actually buzz. Baby steps. No need to rush things along. Save some for another day. Plan.

I like a plan. I Inhale a deep breath, turn around. And freeze. Before I can so much as take a step forward, standing watch across the street, feet planted firmly, I see the dynamic duo, arms crossed, staring me down. Imani uncrosses hers just long enough to make the brusque hand-down wave, the universal signal for get back to it.

I am beaten. I exhale. Turn back around. Buzz.

My buzz is answered by their buzz, and with that, I am in.

The lobby is new, modern, sleek, and rich. Not particularly helpful. Would dingy be better? Hard to say. But the sleekness makes me feel slightly grungy. If I'd known, I would have worn much better shoes, or at least my Sally Ride Vans.

I take the elevator to the sixth floor, drop my backpack for a minute, and clean my glasses. Twice. I make my way down the strategically lit, elegantly appointed hallway to the corner unit. There's a bell, but before I can ring it, the door is opened and she's in front of me. Pale green eyes wide open, her dark hair loose, hanging just below her shoulders. *Zoinks.*

I gulp, but cannot make my brain connect to my hands, never mind how to make them sign. I just stand here and stare. I see a small scar, tiny, white, off the corner of her mouth. Her lips, well they're really nice, boofy.

Mind game moment: I flashback to being fourteen, sitting in the lunchroom. Imani is taking one of those magazine quiz things and she's rattling off what everyone's lips said about them. She had pointed at Eda, who was a senior, and the hottest girl in class, and said, "according to the chart, her larger lower lip means she's a pleasure seeker."

Uh huh. Pleasure seeker. *Wowzerhole.* I just stare.

Maybe for ten seconds. Maybe for thirty. Ava finally breaks the silence, her facial expression turning slightly annoyed, her shoulders scrunching a bit, as her open-palmed hands give a small side-to-side shake, signing "what?"

Which, if I read sign while adding facial expression, is kind of an impatient, "well, what do you want?" and definitely not a "what, OMG, can't believe it's you, how cool is this?"

I somehow connect that I need to stop staring and answer, fumbling, but getting my hands moving long enough to force a sign attempt along the lines of "my name is Sid, and I'd like to ask if you'd maybe go to the movies with me."

My hands feel three sizes too big for my wrists, but I finish and stand there, still out in the hallway, now feeling incredibly awkward. And although I had practiced this sentence an estimated three zillion times, judging from the look on Ava's face, I'm not certain that's what I actually signed.

There is no answer forthcoming, and now it's getting really awkward.

I scrunch up my face and hold out my hands, turning them from palm down to palm up, while I shrug. I'm not sure if I am signing anything pertinent at this point, but I got nothing.

Then she is signing back. Rapidly. And I am lost. Totally. At which point her eyes flicker over me, dismissively. She turns around, and I realize we are not alone. There he is, her friend, Joe. Only now he is looking at me with something like pity and shaking his head.

Ava turns and flashes a handful of signs, rapid-fire, over at him. He answers her just as rapidly, and then they both

16

stand silent. Finally, Joe shrugs and turns toward me. He signs as he speaks.

"She says to tell you asking isn't good enough if you can't understand the answer. But nice try."

My first thought is, "for real?" while my face gets hotter. I think my mouth is actually gaping, but the shock of her casual ingratitude for all my work, my effort, tossing it away like some kind of garbage, is keeping me rooted to the spot even as I wish to move.

I tell myself to pull it together and walk away, go back down the very clean hallway, put one foot in front of the other, when I look up and see, just above Ari, the Brooklyn Bridge visible through the condo's floor to ceiling windows.

Peregrine falcons nest on that bridge. You know they were once nearly extinct in the Eastern US. But they survived. And they thrived.

I meet her eyes, even as I speak carefully to Joe. I use any signs I can kind of figure out. "Tell her I'll be," and then I finger spell, "back."

When I shift my eyes back to Joe to make sure I'm understood, he's grinning and making the universal sign, you know, the one where you take your index fingers and circle around your ear, for crazy.

I have to admit, he's probably not wrong.

THREE

Which is why we, you and I, and Imani, are now in an American Sign Language immersion class, where I am in the process of learning several things.

One, I have hands that don't like to follow directions. My brain says do this and my hands do that. Note to self, pianist is an unlikely career.

Two, Imani has no such challenges. She already speaks six languages fluently, and as I have just said, is rapidly adding a seventh here. And she's beginning her new linguistic journey with every swear word she can think to translate. Which is of no help to me, but does have everyone else charmed. Totally. Current thinking, I hate her.

Three, I will always speak sign language with an accent. I know, who knew?

I'm not talking about ASL vs. BSL a.k.a. British Sign Language. Although I am happy to know that ASL and FSL a.k.a. French Sign Language are similar, thank you, Laurent Clerc. Well, except if you wish to sign *merde*. Then they are completely different in movement.

Nor am I talking about a generational thing, like your parent's idea of hipster anything vs. anyone under the age of twenty!

I'm not even talking about New York accented sign, where yes, you can actually tell which borough someone grew up in with reasonable accuracy.

Nope. It turns out I will always have an "outsider's" accent simply because I didn't grow up speaking sign, and I am a hearing person. And no matter how fluent I become, I will always have a touch of hearing-ese to give me away.

And finally, number four of things I have learned. There are vast cultural gulfs between the hearing and deaf worlds, which I will not detail here other than to say, Alexander Graham Bell.

Yep. Turns out, when Bell set out to invent a telephone, he was not doing it for me or you, but for his wife, his mother, and the family business. Alex, as I like to call him, was an educator of the deaf, son of a deaf woman, married to a deaf woman, and a die-hard oralist, who believed the best way to educate the deaf was to force them to speak and learn how to read lips.

Good old Alex actually supported laws prohibiting the deaf from marrying each other in a belief they might eradicate deafness. Needless to say, Alex is now Mister Bell, and he and I no longer have a loving relationship. Wowzerhole.

Anyway, enough of him.

It might be useful to know there are completely different forms of sign depending on if you use ASL or SEE—which is Signed Exact English—or PSE—which is Pidgin Signed English. Quickly, ASL is its own language, and it's concept based. SEE is sign based upon accurate translation of English, nothing conceptual about it. PSE is a combination generally used by English speakers learning ASL, so it uses ASL signs and grammar, but because a lot of PSE users are from the hearing community in some form, it uses English syntax.

Immersion, we now all understand, is a tricky thing. I'm fingering as fast as I can, so we can all agree I am reasonably fluent in the aforementioned PSE—if I was, oh, maybe, six years old.

However, my classmates and teacher, all of whom

19

learned the highly embellished, dramatically emoted comi-tragic story from Imani, reassure me I should be conversant enough to make another approach.

No. No. No. No.

I can feel you, my friends, wrinkling your noses and scrunching up your faces in what is either massive confusion or apparent disgust, puzzled as to why I'm even bothering. Well, I can lie and say I don't know why either, or I could lie and say I like a challenge, but between us the truth is far more base.

I am simply, *hormonally*, committed to this moment.

Which means I need a plan. Can you say, daunting? So, I think and discard, then Google and discard, until I find what might be a perfect Saturday night date, making it time for me to shut my overthinking brain down and make my move. Again. Well, after I practice. A lot.

Okay, maybe obsessively. Hey, it didn't go so well last time. So yes, a lot. With Imani, Jimmy, Ari, Vikram, and anyone else I can find to "chat" with me. It is the first thing I do in the morning, and the last thing I do in bed while falling asleep at night. Sweet dreams are definitely not made of this . . .

. . . Date. Take both hands and form the letter "d," which is a circle with a raised index finger. Then take both "d's" and have the circle parts meet each other in the middle. Okay.

Now connect Date to Roller Derby. "D's" to bent "V" hands, palms facing up, each in front of either side of my chest. Now moving them forward and back with an alternating swinging movement, then finger spell d-e-r-b-y.

Yes. Roller Derby. Girls on skates. Moving fast.

The Gotham Girls are a founding member league of the Women's Flat Track Derby Association, and a spinning, spiraling, jamming, blocking, elbow-throwing group of awesomeness.

Tonight's match is the Manhattan Mayhem vs. the

Brooklyn Bombshells. And it's happening at the John Jay College gym.

For the uninitiated, in an aside of perfection, John Jay College was founded as the only liberal arts college in the US with a criminal justice and forensic focus. Which tickles all my Velma bones no end.

And it's located at 524 West Fifty-Ninth. Right in Midtown Manhattan. Which makes it super easy for everyone to get to.

I mean so perfect, right?

And as for roller derby? Come on, it fits my politics, my ideals, and my outsized fantasy of myself as a would-be jammer/warrior out there flying by on those skates, deking to the left, ducking to the right, score! IRL I think we can all guess I probably would not be overly happy with other people's elbows flying at my face, but in my mind I am jamming.

Well if not jamming, I am definitely, officially, flying. Off the wall. Off the tracks. Off the cuff. Off the rails. Well, not off the rails yet. That's coming . . .

SHE SAYS YES.

. . . and it's here!

I am now officially off the charts, the rails, the map!

My besties spring into action. A flurry of texts and I have both rounded up the troops and worked out an appropriate wardrobe. The latter part has less to do with me, and more to do with Imani's, "what are you wearing?"

The result? I am nattily attired with black wing-tip Commanders, black jeans, with a white T-shirt and my favorite vest. I swiped Jimmy's old varsity jacket from him a couple of years ago, because apparently it looks cool on me. Or so I'm told. I thought I would wear a sweater, but I apparently thought wrong.

According to Imani, and confirmed by Ari, "When the action gets going it will be too hot for a sweater, but you'd be stuck, because taking it off would reveal a now sweaty, slept-in looking T-shirt, which would totally destroy the look."

Although I have an instinctive moment of need to respond with something snarky like "totes," it is astonishingly followed by a moment of rethink, and to the audible relief of my personal fashionistas, I simply concur. Hey, tonight, I am not going to risk anything impinging on my cool vibe. And it is pretty amazing listening to them think through an outfit three steps ahead. Jacket it is.

For a finishing touch, we agreed on my *très*-retro analog watch with its big black cuff band. Actually, I'm not sure we agreed. Exactly. I think Imani just gave in. But this was a birthday gift from my Dad and, yes, it's big. It's really a men's watch, but it's got this great five-pointed star in the face, and I love it more than Imani does.

I have to say, creating an entire outfit for Comic-Con was less terrifying than this.

Before leaving, I check myself out in the mirror, and while taking a deep breath to theoretically calm my nerves I do have to marvel how impressive it is that Imani can do all this via text.

And then I'm off. I hook up with the gang outside the arena. Vik's already picked up everyone's tickets, so I fork over some cash, take mine and Ava's and Joe's, and shoo them off, reluctantly, truculently, to get good seats.

Left alone, I do what I do best. Pace. I pause, glance around, nothing. I pace some more. And this time, when I turn back around, Ava and Joe emerge from the subway. And even wrapped up in a coat and scarf against the night chill, she takes my breath away.

I sign hi, but not much else, as we make our way inside, muscling through the crowd just as the game is starting. And I'm hyper-conscious about everything, but particularly how loud and raucous it all is, and how as the skaters are pounding the track it vibrates the room.

All things I never gave any thought to. Until tonight. Because tonight, well, tonight is different. Tonight, all I can think about is her nearness.

The skaters go by, and the rush of their adrenaline mixes with my adrenaline, and I wonder if Ava feels them, or feels all the energy pouring off me, vibrating with that same rush of power the skaters exude.

And then Manhattan scores big on a jam, the place explodes, and our hands brush as we stand up to glimpse the action. My knees buckle; my pulse jumps. Is it by accident, or by design?

I feel light-headed, caught somewhere between pleasantly buzzed and rip-roaring drunk. I can feel my heart thumping, my pulse erratic, my body sending waves of heat as though it is thrusting me forward.

Until somehow we are walking home. And the group keeps moving one step faster than us until they are six or seven steps ahead. And then they are eight or nine, and those green eyes turn to look at me.

I don't know who moves first.

But there is a shop, an alcove, whose door is closed, wrought iron gate pulled across, and that's all we need to know. Hands grab jackets and push and pull until we are tucked away from the street. And I search her face, watch those pale green eyes darkening, almost becoming the sea on a stormy night. And they're pulling me into her, and I know she's hungry. I know she's hungry, exactly the way I'm hungry. Needy, the way I'm needy.

And she's here. And I'm here.

I hesitate for an agonizing second, drinking her in, letting her lips move the slightest bit toward me until I am closing the gap, and even though I know it's happening, it still takes me a minute to realize I am kissing her.

Gently. Is it a question? So very gently. Is it permission?

The soft pressure increases. The answer is there as she kisses me back. I feel her hand flutter upward, burning me as she touches my skin. I lean into that touch, a low groan of pleasure rumbling up from deep within.

My hand buries itself in Ava's hair. Twisting. Twining. She pulls back slightly, leaving me a moment to inhale its scent. Her scent. My entire body is a shaking mess, my knees threatening to buckle.

What is too fast? What is too slow?

I am fighting for air, and she pulls me back to her, her hands now tugging at the short ends of my hair, and I am lost, knowing without thought, only knowing that I can no longer breathe on my own, but only through her mouth.

I want more, need more, but before I can shift, I hear it.

Or more accurately, them.

It's a startling cacophony of catcalls, one of which instructs us, gleefully, to "get a room!"

Crashing back to reality, pulling rapidly away, my heart pounds from a mixture of lust and fear. I never heard them coming.

I glance over at my so-called friends—although since Joe is right there in the midst, I think I can say *our* so-called friends. It's impressive how without even knowing some of the signs Joe is flashing I am able to fully interpret their meaning.

Seems my potentially former friends backtracked and are now huddled together on the sidewalk, laughing, jeering, and raising their hands, shaking them in the air—the sign for applause—all with one shared goal, our total humiliation.

Which is working. I am seized by mortification, followed by a rush of defensive annoyance, when I feel Ava hiding in my T-shirt, shaking with laughter. And everyone else recedes. This is everything, and it's not enough.

And as the obscene gestures, hoots, and howls continue to not impress, I am bombarded with conflicting thoughts. First, how on occasion it must be really nice to not hear anything and just have the world tuned out. But, it's immediately pushed aside by the second, how frightening that must be and how vulnerable this leaves a person.

I feel my arm wrap around her, tightening just a bit.

FOUR

"Bonne après-midi."

Uh oh. She is sitting in the kitchen, at the small bistro table, and is using the French good afternoon, rather than an English good morning. French. Not English. Delivered in mother tone—the one that instantly lets me know I have slept way later than I realize.

It's also the tone that reminds me of Oscar Wilde's quote, "sarcasm is the lowest form of wit." It's a personal fav. Well, unless of course it's aimed at me. And yes, I know there is some debate as to whether or not Oscar actually said this, which if he didn't, he should have, so that's good enough for me. Not that it particularly matters at this point. The tone has its intended effect. My hand freezes reaching for the coffeepot.

Maman's right eyebrow rises over her cup. "Shall I take it you had a good night last night?"

Now, I would love to report I played it cool. That I was completely chill, cavalier about the whole thing, or at least coy, or even perhaps cloaked, but the minute she asked, my face broke into a huge, stupid grin, so I am forced to admit I folded like a cheap suit.

But at least I am smart enough to not start talking. If I start, I am not going to stop, and that would be humiliating.

Instead, I switch gears, forget about the coffee, reach into the fridge, grab a yogurt, rip off its lid, and shove a spoonful into my mouth. Only then do I look up, do that grin/shrug

26

thing, turn and go for the hasty exit before I have a chance to swallow and she has a chance to get another question out.

There might have been a chuckle following me as I high-tailed it down the hallway. I shall neither confirm nor deny.

I shall, however, return to the safety of my bedroom . . .

. . . or so I think. Because while I was happily sleeping away, which let's be honest, did not occur until sometime deep in the wee hours of the morning, other people were rising and shining. Until then, when they had presumably been happily sleeping, I had been seriously very wide-awake, replaying every inch of my evening over and over and over again, which, for the record, was a lot of replay. Therefore, they are now happily awake and furiously messaging me.

I scroll the list. It is endless, filled with everyone's need to know.

Well everyone except one.

And yes, this would normally be my crazy-making spot, dwelling incessantly on what this very particular lack of communication could, in fact, mean. Only I'm not. I am not consumed by anxiety because I am assuming my lack of text from Ava is from a similarly exhausted, and yet bliss-filled, night.

Why such sudden adulting?

Because standing here, echoing still, on a continuous loop in my head is the now-added mental musical accompaniment of Shakira, telling me hips don't lie.

And that's only half of it. Oh yeah. Neither do lips.

Exhaling, I shake my head, stick the spoon in my mouth, grab my phone, prop up my pillows, and climb back into bed.

Where you might assume I busied myself responding. Errant assumption.

In my defense, I did take a short stab at responsible responding. I clicked on Jimmy's first, because his was unsurprisingly at the top of the list, only to find an MP3 waiting for me.

27

I roll my eyes, but go ahead and hit play. I hear the opening chords of Kehlani's "Honey." By the time she sings the part about the *beautiful wreck/colorful mess/but I'm funny*, even knowing fully well this was sent to tease me, I am incapable of stopping my reaction, which, while it has nothing to do with any pranking he may have been thinking, is still torturous.

I let my phone fall to the wayside as Kehlani's bed of acoustic guitar chords mingles with whispers of my memories, and together they begin rhythmically teasing me, taunting me, beckoning me.

I don't bother fighting. Nope. I succumb to their power and resume my state of self-induced floating on air. Which for a wee while keeps my mind wonderfully occupied.

The next few hours pass in a whirlwind of emotion. I am jubilant, aroused, relishing how when I lie still, close my eyes, I can actually, physically, feel her lips.

The pings continue; however, because I can identify each one, they are no more than a faint background tone to be ignored. None of them are hers.

But as I feel her lips, I caress this union, believing we are equally entwined in a memory of erotic phantasmic proportions.

Minutes turn to hours, and even phantasm cannot be sustained. At some point, even an illusionary likeness needs feeding. By the time six o'clock rolls around, my hunger is raging. I am beside myself and have definitely turned on Shakira and her thinking.

The earlier texts, that barrage of "how was it," I managed, in between lolling, gasping, and dreaming, to answer with various forms of "amazing," be it in words or emoticons or gifs. New messages ping "well?" implying I should have a plan, a next thrill to share, and for this I have no answers.

By my count, I have about thirty minutes before a parent will expect my appearance to help with dinner, and all I have to show for my day is the figurative skin I am crawling out of.

Shakira is wrong. It seems hips, and lips, do lie.

Deflation is an incredibly painful thing. It's like all the cells in my body are shrinking down, eating into themselves, feasting upon my sadness.

"Sidonie?"

The call is faint, but I hear it. I don't need to answer. It's the dinner help yell. I wish I had a good excuse to ignore it, but I don't want to talk about it, so I don't bother to try.

I stand up, put my phone down, put my eyeglasses on. I don't even care that they are smudged. I take a deep breath, let it out as a choking sigh, and leave the room. My walk has turned from victory to shame, a small journey of apparent palpability because by the time I reach the kitchen, Mom and Dad are suddenly very busy with their chopping and dicing, leaving me alone to quietly set the table.

The quiet continues unabated.

Until, somehow, it is Monday morning. And my palpability seemingly travels, as evidenced by a waiting Imani and Ari. No Jimmy. No Vik. Just the two of them.

I walk gingerly up to meet them, afraid of what they will say, afraid of how I must seem today, shrunken and depleted. They say nothing, but turn so I am positioned between them. And they walk me to school, providing me the silent support of the girlfriend type. A procession, a vigil, a ritual whether standing or sitting or walking or weeping we keep for each other when we need it.

When we need it, I realize with a shock, is when we are ghosted.

"Ghosted." I say it out loud, even as I try to absorb its meaning, just as we arrive at the steps. "I have been ghosted."

Imani puts her head on my right shoulder as Ari wraps her right arm through my left elbow. And just like that they usher me up the stairs.

Upon arrival, my silent support team expands to four and maintains itself throughout the day. But when school lets out, I know it is time for me to work this out for myself. So, with hugs all around, I head out. And just as I am determining which view will be prove the best High Line safety/thinking seat, my phone pings with a new text.

It's a GIF. It's written in lipstick and says "I want to kiss all over you." And then lipstick lips pop up one after another until the screen is covered in kisses.

I take it in with my eyes, but feel it with my groin. The lower half of my body squirms painfully, then pleasurably, then repeat.

The GIF gave way to a message: Tomorrow. After school. My apartment.

And just like that, ghosting is gone, swept away in an instant, replaced by light and warmth and something like relief. It's heady and giddy and knee-weakening. It's as if the universe took a deep bow replete with a big sweeping flourish and said, *Sidonie Rubin, you've won a week to remember.*

Or at the very least, a Tuesday.

I arrive a little later than I want. By the time school lets out and I get a train to DUMBO, it's nearly four. So I run as fast as I can, suddenly hating their quaint cobblestones, but still make it from the station to the building in record time. Then, right as I am about to pull open the glass doors to the vestibule, I slow my roll and try to find my balance.

I let go of the handle, standing outside the entry, remembering the last time I was here. Which did not go well.

But that time, I just showed up. This time, she did ask me. I am an invited guest.

And I reach for the right-side metal door handle. Before I pull it open, forty thousand thoughts have grabbed on and take off running, each trying to scramble a route through my mind until we have a winner. Maybe I should have changed my outfit, maybe I should have gotten my hair cut, maybe I should have studied up on how to sign "you look great."

As the beat-the-brain race continues, an older woman exits the building, pausing to scrutinize me with the suspicious "do I let her in, do I call the police" side-eye. I give her what I hope is a reassuring slight head nod, small grin attempt, trying not to look threatening, which seems to work because she moves on, but not before she checks the inner door has closed with me still on the outside.

Which is perfect timing for my winning thought, racing across the finish line, ready to announce itself to me. Yes folks, it's my alter ego, the "kazoo" voice. *She didn't actually say anything to you other than come over. It doesn't mean she's interested.*

Wow. I so did not see that one sneaking ahead.

Yeah, well, Her GIF did come in lipstick and it did say she wants to kiss me all over. And she didn't have to text. She could have just left us in silence mode until all my, what was that expression Ze uses, oh yeah my qi, until all my qi, all the energy that powers my body and spirit, ebbed away.

Duck a fluck, Sid. We are not doing this. Take a deep breath. Now pull on your big girl pants. Pull open the doors. Scan the tenant list, and ring the damn bell.

What can I say? Loudest voice wins.

I reach out, pull open the door, enter vestibule, and buzz. And I wait. Maybe two seconds, maybe three. I am buzzed in.

FIVE

She's waiting for me as I exit the elevator. She signs hello, and I sign back. As we walk, Ava begins to sign not exactly an apology, but more like her story, to me. I don't get all of it, just bits and pieces.

I manage to grasp that I was unexpected for her. A full hearing person with no ties to the deaf community. At first, she said, she laughed me off. Approaching her at the robotics competition, I was a flattering moment, and it was sweet. And that was that. Or it should have been. Only it wasn't. Because then I went and I found her.

I tracked her down just as I had promised. And while that was kind of shocking, it was still easy to take the action as a compliment and move along. Only then I came back. And by now, Ava had to admit she was shocked, but also impressed and, well, flattered by how hard I had worked.

And yet, even as she said yes to roller derby, even then, Ava said she didn't expect to find me ... Her hands trail off as she pauses, searching for something, which I have to say is helpful, allowing me a too brief moment to play catch up.

My head is spinning, both from the strain of trying to translate a language I don't speak well, and then trying to process what she is telling me, because it's important and not just some line or two of gossip I am missing out on.

We've reached her apartment door. Ava turns to me, and for the first time signs very carefully, deliberately, watching to make sure I can interpret her.

"You are unexpected. And," Ava's hands go still for just a second before she points her index finger at me, followed by her fist closing and then reopening with her fingers splayed outward, over her breast, until they finally turn back to point to herself, "you scare me."

I scare her?

Oh. Wow. I don't know what I'm supposed to say or feel or even do with that one. Thankfully it seems my stunned face is enough. Ava continues to stare, but also reaches back to open the door.

Her hand grasps the knob; then she seems to have a change of heart, and her hand comes forward one more time, open palm across her chest as she begins "My . . ."

I watch her dance rapidly through several signs, but I'm already overloaded and definitely not catching what she is saying. I am catching that she looks rather fetching. I like fetching. It has a nice coyness to it.

And score one for an absolutely epic multitask. Despite my inability to knowingly focus on anything other than how perfectly poofed Ava's lips appear, my fingers manage to miraculously be replaying a few signs down low, repeating them for me until I can consciously pay them any mind.

Ava looks at me quizzically for just a brief second, laughs, leans down, grabs my hand, and pulls me through the door.

Where I can now look around at something other than her mouth, while my hand, which has continued its refrain, open hand, thumb to chin, bump up to forehead, begins to connect. Wait. I know I know this one. Think. Mom and Dad . . . Parents! Got it. "My parents," hand sweep into letter "s" fists, tapping one over the other. "Work!" Exactly.

Great. I am now trying to remember the other signs and suddenly two plus two do make four. And I blush, a rush of heat everywhere. *My parents are working; we're the only ones here.*

I turn, as though mesmerized by the bridge view showcased through those floor-to-ceiling windows. It is *entre chien et loup.* The sun is just lowering in the sky. The red, fiery ball sinks another inch lower. *It is the time between dog and wolf.*

We are the only ones here.

I stare out at the sun, watching it drop, trying to wrap my brain around this now decoded piece of information. WWSSD? What would Suave Sid do? What should Suave Sid do? Suave Sid who?

Ava presses against me from behind, slipping her arms through my elbows until her hands are in front of me, where she points a finger back at me—"you." Her fingers now switch to a sort of thumbs up. *I rock?* Maybe. I try mentally reversing the position to me, but since I can feel Ava pressing up against me, that's pretty much useless.

Right hand moves two fingers left, H, followed by left hand moving to a circle, O, and then right hand puts a thumb below index finger while hand is in a fist, T. *I rock hot?*

Ava's arms pull back until her hands are lightly touching right above my breasts, then they pull down rapidly.

Forget thinking, I am gasping, as she spins me around and pulls me to her until my lips find hers. And just as I lean in, she steps back, looks me in the eye and grabs my hand.

Body! That's what that means! *I rock a hot body!* Or something like that.

Her bedroom is an array of oranges. Bright. Emotional. A tapestry of sunrises and sunsets. I turn and Ava's gaze is directly focused on my lips; like the colors surrounding me, it's fiery. And it's hungry. And yet, as she closes the gap between us, she gives one oddly gentle pause, and suddenly I'm reaching, closing, needing.

We fall into the bed, my hand buries itself in her hair, tilting her head back up to me. Ava arches her back, thrusting herself ever closer toward me. My denim clad leg shifts between her thighs, until finally we become one breath, one body.

SIX

It's dark, not particularly late, but the sun is long gone when I exit the building. It's a wickedly beautiful night. I'm smiling at the city view ahead, walking without feeling the pavement. Floating on air, I am so high.

Me and my exciting new rhythm accompanist, Bruno Mars, are apparently both reviewing the possibility of marriage, as we rock our way down the block, off to grab the subway. And while he's singing, amazingly right on beat I'm thinking maybe, Ava, I will marry you. Drum pound around. I execute a more or less Milly Rock'ish move. Look up and freeze. Heading down the same block I am now dancing up, I spy an apparition in the guise of Ari and Imani.

Although I must say, for an apparition, they are looking a bit chilled. Why it's almost as though they're really flesh and blood, and have been out here waiting for a while, fake chillaxing. Which of course, they have. Because this is what one might call an ambush.

Not that this deduction requires anywhere near a Sherlock Holmesian intellect. From my personal Ava infatuation experience, I know exactly what they've been up to. They've been sitting outside on the West Elm rooftop, indulging in way too much caffeine, waiting to catch sight of me exiting the building, fully planning to cut me off on my way to the train.

I give them credit; it's a solid plan.

"Well?" Ari demands, before her feet actually stop

walking forward. She might even be described as half a block away.

Music stops. Feet land hard. Crash landing back on planet Earth is now complete.

Which I know because even in my not-so-in-it, actually-slightly-still-out-of-it state of mind, I instinctively find I am looking around suspiciously.

"They're not here," Imani says moving fast, still raising her voice as she closes the distance. An annoyed man grunts as he zigzags his way around me, only to then run into her. That elicits a minor rambling curse. We both ignore him.

"Jimmy and Vik can get the nicely sanitized it-was-great version." She pauses for a minute, switching from loud and matter-of-fact to something stage-whispery-playful-coy. "Well, was it?"

Sometimes her theatrical talents are annoying.

I don't answer immediately. I do blush, which I try to cover by pulling my jacket tighter and wrapping my arms around my body. Protective? Maybe. As we clog the side-walk, another annoyed body pushes by. As though on cue, we fling our fake-smile, quasi grimace, all sarcasm at him.

"Oh please," Imani's now all business, laughing, perhaps even scoffing, at my feeble attempt at ignoring her. "We are being so incredibly polite."

"And gentle." Ari catches up, just in time to hear Imani's reply, and immediately chimes in. Beat not missed.

"Now Sid, there's no reason to make this an inquisition. We all know, a) friends tell friends, and b)," Imani pauses for a pitying look. "You honestly do have the worst poker face ever put on the planet."

This provokes a snort of laughter from Ari, who holds up her hand for the requisite high-five moment.

And while I would love to protest, claim I am being unfairly targeted, I cannot. Alas, it is true. I do have the worst poker face ever. But I still hesitate. I'm not sure I'm ready to share anything. On the other hand, now that they're here and they've asked, you know, it is intoxicating to think about sharing *something*. But which parts?

My mind begins replaying my last few hours, and just as I feel myself begin to smile I hear it.

"Sidonie's got a girlfriend, Sidonie's got a girlfriend." It's a low singsong emanating from my right. I freeze. But that doesn't stop the heat flushing up my face.

Holy mortification, Batman! From the shadows about three doors away, the taunter saunters, slowly taking shape, revealing an enthusiastically, broadly grinning, up to his elbows in roguish self-satisfaction, Jimmy. He's accompanied by a decidedly less-grinning Vik.

While they slither up, I unfreeze long enough to wheel accusingly at Imani and Ari, only to see them standing there, equally appalled. And yes, there is some irony there.

Ari attacks first, "Vik. What the fuck?!"

For the briefest of seconds it looks as though Vik is going to answer her, when instead he sinks slightly lower, shoving his hands into his pockets, and head bobs over at Jimmy.

I appreciate Ari's thrust, I do. But I know Vik will not parry. Why? Because I already know Vik has nothing to do with this. Zero. Zilch. This genius junior high move has James I-have-known-you-since-pre-K Flynn written all over it.

And just like that it's game on.

"Now, Sid," Mr. Five Fingers Flynn, quarterback extraordinaire, begins, looking up from his pocket, keeping on his toes, working on where he will throw this particular ball. Is it a handoff, a short pass, going deep? Given Vik's cower, I'm ruling out the handoff.

I watch him through what I like to think are my "hooded eyes" as he checks down.

"I am hurt. Crushed." Jimmy closes the space between us. *One.* "I have known you the longest of all of us." Step closer. *Two.* "I have supported you through good times and bad." Step. *Three.* "From kindergarten to our senior year of high

38

school." Step again. *Hut.* "And that should mean something." *Hut.*

Jimmy pauses, his focus intense as he takes one last step so we are now only inches apart, "And, even more sad, I would not expect such a show of blatant discrimination from you of all people." *Hut.*

My head jerks up, screaming "incoming."

"Let's be honest, if you had a gay *guy* best friend, he would have been waiting outside the apartment, and that would have been not just perfectly acceptable, it might even have been expected." *Release. Going deep.*

It's a perfect spiral, thrown straight to the end zone. Not a defender in sight. Jimmy and I stand there, toe to toe, his smile gaining cockiness by the second.

Touchdown.

Just like he drew it up.

The crowd goes wild. Five Fingers Flynn scores again.

I look at Jimmy. My lips are pursed. My head shakes. "Oh my God, you are such an asshole." I hit his shoulder, but he doesn't even flinch. Instead he wraps me up in a big hug, ignoring my squirms to get away.

Through smushed face and glasses, I look around at the gang, trying futilely to ignite annoyance. But we're all laughing, and then we're off.

Platitudes awaits.

And I'm sure you can all imagine how that goes. It is at least a double basket of fries. Might even be a triple.

And while dodging the playful, annoying interrogation, I suddenly realize I actually can't tell them much because I don't have words. I know, shocking. Yes, I know a lot of words, but not of the romantic descriptor category. I can do sappy, and I can do drippy, and I can do eye-rolling, but I can't find vocabulary to share the joy and exhilaration and wonder of my day.

I can't even fathom that it was today. That it was only three hours ago.

39

But I know there are words. There are lots of words. I just need to find them.

And I do, sometime around Wednesday, at approximately, oh, three o'clock in the morning, find the ones I seek. The ones fit for my immediate needs. It's a quote. It says it's from Dr. Seuss. Before you snort and say, "of course," it doesn't actually have attribution, so that part's kind of iffy. But whoever really did write it down, I thank them.

"You know you're in love when you can't fall asleep because reality is finally better than your dreams."

Yeah, I know. Words. Perfect words.

And no, I won't use them for Mr. Clifton's final exam, the one where we submit our favorite quote. Some things aren't meant for sharing. They are just for the knowing. And, then again, some things, sometimes, are meant for the sharing. At least a tidbit's worth. Or two. Or forty-seven.

I am surviving our first four days of what I believe are official dating, although I'm not quite sure how. It's hard to fathom how I'm supposed to function when my brain is driven by only one thought—fist with thumb on the outside, victory sign, fist with thumb on the outside a.k.a.—AVA.

By the time Thursday comes, I am running late and on fumes. I haven't been able to see her all week. I won't see her after school today. Or tomorrow. She has some presentation she has to do. I may die.

Alternatively my friends may kill me. It would be a mercy killing. A jury of their actual peers would not convict.

Okay, so maybe I am suddenly a little bit chatty about everything. Isn't that what they all wanted? Demanded even. Details, Sid!

So I provided them—over and over and over again. It's not like they haven't shared their emotive harangues from time to time.

But still, Radio WSID in New York City?

Yes, the latest bout of purportedly good-natured hijinks

begins with none other than Vikram Patel on the front steps to school, his hand cupped around half his mouth, using a radio voice I totally didn't even know he had.

"Welcome to WSID in New York City, Cooper's very own oldies station. Today, our number one with a bullet is a song first recorded in1962 by Gene Chandler, Schmoop of Earl, presented here, live, featuring our very own Coopertonix."

Okay. I can admit this would have been genius if it had been my idea.

But it wasn't. And the aforementioned "today's number one" was actually yesterday's. Today, even though I'm not here yet, because I'm running late, they are not deterred. Apparently, the show will go on.

Imani, of course, has lead vocals, so as I turn the corner, I find them gleefully harmonizing away. *Hang on Schmoopie, Schmoopie hang on.* And oh, great, looks like Marcus is now a member, bringing his mad beatboxer skills, to this seemingly inspired rendition from the Coopertonix. I am judging this to be a smash hit from the crowd outside, which, as I make my way through the gates, is growing.

Along with the hilarity factor, also growing . . . old. Fast.

And of course, I am spotted. Janelle, our very own mouth of the south, queen of the mean, is saying something and pointing toward me. Which is my cue to fake a grin, pretend to be completely amused, do the head bob thing and force-laugh my way forward.

I also spot Scott Olney, standing near the edge of the crowd, watching me with a look akin to sympathy. Or maybe just pity. Let me be clear, anyone whose nickname up until very recently has been jack-off is not allowed to be sympathetic. Even if I like him better than I did, we're still not that close.

Note to self: get that fake grin cooking. Maybe even a high five or a shoulder punch as I head up the steps. Might even have to sprint up.

Because if I'm being frank, or even jane—pause for the cheap chortle—I know, my choices suck. I can run home and curl up in a ball, or launch another frantic round of cleaning, emailing, Google-ating, snapchatting, etc.

My life is becoming a debacle waiting to happen. Worse. It's becoming a public debacle.

And cue the PING.

Saturday. 9. Penn Station. Wear your wingtips. Surprise.

SEVEN

Which I nearly totally blow. I mean, how was I supposed to know 9 on Saturday was 9:00 A.M., as in nine o'clock in the morning? I don't use the twenty-four-hour clock. I just assumed she meant Saturday night!

And yes, I do know what they say about assume; that it makes an ass of u and me. Thanks for that.

Anyway, it was the morning teasing chat of the snap with pic of the tix that clued me in, hard and fast.

Washington, DC?

Wowzerhole. Panic rising.

Grab wallet, grab coat, scream, "Later," while flying out the door. Feet don't fail me now. Gasp. Run. Gasp. Run.

Down Seventh. Over toward Thirty-First. Cross over. Head down. Thirteen minutes to get there. Pull up. Hate idiots who don't know to stay to the right if they're not walking the escalator. *Merde*, people! Jump up. Slide the banister down. Welcome to the busiest station in North America. Swim the sea of humanity, maneuver through the peeps without tripping them or me. And there it is. The Amtrak area.

Breathless. I've made it. And she's waiting in line. "Yeah," I am nearly doubled over, panting while signing "I'm fine, Ava, I'm fine."

And I am. I'm here and I've made it and I don't know how, but I have. And Ava is as fabulous as I have imagined all week. And as I look up and see her smile, but before I

43

decide if I should kiss her, or at least give her a hug, or do something other than stare, they're calling the train, our train, and we're on the move.

Two coach seats, side by side, hands entwined, watching the world go by. Ava looks out the window, but occasionally turns back to me. And after a week spent in a near constant state of arousal, I find I am oddly calm, happy just having her next to me, just being able to sit watching her. Until it's "Baltimore. Next stop, Washington, DC."

I let Ava know we're next, somewhat regretfully. I mean it's great that our adventure has begun, but I've found a sweet spot breathing in the scent of Ava's shampoo or conditioner, almost an aphrodisiac by itself, and the motion gently rocking.

All that's missing is a door I can pull shut.

Fortunately, Ava was not watching my face on that thought, saved by the old pulling into Union Station screech. She was busy reaching overhead for her backpack when the train did its hit-the-brakes-jar-the-people, so I now gallantly reach overhead and grab her backpack, using the train jolt to hide behind while I gather my emotions back together.

The pack is stuffed full, and to effortlessly hoist and toss it on behind me takes slightly more effort, with lots less grace, than I had imagined. But Ava leans over to adjust the strap and gives me a quick kiss, so I know not only did my gallantry not go unnoticed, but I also know the slight twinge in my shoulder was worth every twist.

I ignore the pleasure/pain even a simple kiss is generating in favor of both not embarrassing us and getting us off. The train!

We grab smoothies inside the station as Ava shares more of our plans, telling me we are heading over to her friend Emma's dorm room at Gallaudet University. But we're early, so we've got time to go to the National Mall and walk the Sculpture Garden.

44

Which is what we do, holding hands, looking at art, and walking. And I'm torn. Part of me wants to ask questions, but a bigger part of me never wants to let go of her hand, so mostly I'm quiet.

And quiet is hard. I'm used to talking a mile a minute, sharing amazing tidbits of trivia or trying to think up scathingly witty remarks, or even just scathing ones, and sometimes, on occasion, succeeding. Here I'm not sure what to do. I just don't want to do it wrong.

The pop art Roy Lichtenstein house nearly distracts, but not quite. And I do love Roxy Paine's *Graft*, which has a long explanation, but mostly makes me think of the *Wizard of Oz* and flying monkeys.

And slowly we are coming full circle, making our way toward the exit, and I glance back and see Hector Guimard's *An Entrance to the Paris Metropolitain*. And something about Paris and art nouveau, and finally I can't.

I let Ava get a half step in front of me, pull her hand back, lock eyes, and then step toward her. Still locked on her eyes, I lean in and give her the kiss I've needed to. It's only then, when her lips meet mine, that I close my eyes, and only for the briefest of moments. Somehow, I manage to remember we are in a public place. And somehow I step back.

As I release her, I bring my hand up to her cheek and gently spell A V A.

Hands now entwined from the arms, we head to Emma's room, and find a note on the door, "key in room 23." I take off the backpack, set it down next to me and wait, leaning against a wall, while Ava goes to find the room and retrieve the key.

Two women come down the hallway, hands flying through the air, their faces reflecting, steering their signing choices, obviously deep in conversation. They give me a casual once-over, but keep moving.

Ava returns, unlocks the door, and with a sweeping

motion ushers us both inside. I grab the backpack and enter. In one surprisingly efficient move, Ava takes it and tosses it aside, closing the door.

And no one's home, and her lips are on mine, and mine are on hers, and we are leaning against the now-closed door, engaged in an epic tongue-of-war, and I don't care who wins or loses.

We're gonna go with it was a draw.

Then, as we're snuggled on the bed, Ava unveils our plans. Which include a party off-campus tonight. Late. Very. Ava motions at her bag, at the room, until her hands splay at me, nice and wide. She might as well be screaming, "Slumber Party!" or maybe just, "Duh! What did you think was going on!"

Oh boy. Double wowzer.

I lunge for my phone and begin texting. First Imani: "staying your house tonight. k?"

It takes approximately two seconds for the ping back: "k"

I now consternate, trying to think what exactly I shall say to Mom, other than "staying at Imani's." It's not that I never lie to my parents, hello, you've been there. It's that I try and stick with things like omission and not deliberate choice. Big exhale. Hands run through short, now sticking up, hair.

I watch Ava watching me as I slowly piece together enough vocabulary to sign something resembling, "easier, tell me, plan," I hope. I'm not sure about my "plan" sign.

She holds her hands flat, with her palms up, and then does a kind of seesaw thing where one hand raises while the other lowers. Her face kind of matches the movements, a little pouty lip, a slight left-right head toss. *Maybe.*

And then she is pulling a big fake frown, as her hands move until finally both hands lie flat, make a fist, her index and middle fingers extend together. She leaves her left hand chest-high, flat while her right hand goes up to her nose, touches it, and then moves down to touch her left hand. *Fun.*

Not as much fun.

And that kind of summed it up, fun, and not as much fun. Mostly, I think, because everything was different, and in some ways exhausting, and in others exhilarating.

It begins with Ava unpacking that backpack. She brought clothes for the party, for us both. And she looks amazing, in a black miniskirt, with a tight turtleneck that matches her eyes, and thigh-high boots. Point for exhilarating.

For me, she brought a shirt, with a tie, or an ascot, or a cravat, or a something. I'm not really sure, but when put on, her shirt choice is all very *Gentleman Jack*. That show about Anne Lister stars the amazing, stunning, be-still-my-heart Suranne Jones and features an awesome wardrobe by Tom Pye. But that hair kind of scares me.

Yeah. I know. But I am *not* digressing. I have gotten much better about that. Right now I'm actually stalling.

It's funny. When I cosplay, I love it. It's this awesome, artistic, I don't know, thing. But when I'm cosplaying, I choose the person I become. And yes, this outfit would have looked awesome back when we, the fab five, investigated our way into that steampunk LARP. But that was my choice. Okay, yes, I will grant you, with a lot of help from Imani.

And it's taken me a long time to incorporate even pieces of my butch truth into public, as exceptionally sharply turned-out as it might be honestly.

But I choose those. This feels, I would imagine, like putting on too much makeup. You know, it's not that a person wouldn't wear that eyeliner or lipstick, but they might not wear it to, I dunno, the church social. Although granted, since I've never been to a church social, that's a slightly preconceived notion.

My point is, being dressed like this for a party in a roomful of people I don't know, is not exactly comfortable.

I know, controlling much.

As for the party itself, it's way off-campus, taking about forty-five minutes to find, and it's packed, wild, and, surprisingly for me, incredibly loud. I motion to Ava, pointing first at my ear, then shaking my fists.

She glances around, shrugs, "I guess." But she keeps looking at me; then a small smile forms, a small head cock to the right, pause, and she signs, "That's what all you hearing people say."

She watches me translate, throws back her head laughing, and drags me onto the dance floor.

The rest of the night's a blur, and by the time we get back to the room, at whatever ridiculous hour that was, I'm definitely beyond tipsy and beyond exhausted. But there's no sign of Emma, and Ava presses her body next to mine, releasing my tie, then taking her left hand and holding it on my chest, while with her right hand she makes a small "d," which she then wipes quickly before my face. She then changes to form an "x" which she starts at her cheekbone, moves to her chin, and then changes to a "y."

Damn. Sexy.

And just like that, exhaustion passes, and I am back once again, exhilarating. Oh yeah!

The next morning, a.k.a. maybe two hours later, we wake up and head to Starbucks. Right down the block from Gallaudet is Starbucks' first US signing store, and yep, right beneath its signature sign, etched or decaled onto the windows, is S-T-A-R-B-U-C-K-S, all finger spelled. Ava walks herself right up and signs our order, turns to me with a grin, and I realize it's something so simple, something I do every day, and yet something she can't do everywhere she goes.

I go grab us two seats and think I should be floating on air or, given my lack of sleep, hovering above the sidewalk, but instead I'm truly overwhelmed, taken by sensory overload on so many levels. Especially the need to use my face. In sign, facial expressions are everything. No one can hear you intone "droll" or "icily" or "enthusiastically," so one sign can have different meanings and the person signing must convey the one, the intonation, they want.

I feel like my face is one big fake tic of self-conscious bad acting.

Ava arrives bearing gifts, and as I take the coffee I smile a bit tiredly. By the time we are heading back on the train, I sit quietly, completely traveled out. I take her hand and the miles go by. I suddenly realize it's more than just "traveled out." I am talked out. Which might just be a first. I have been, as Robert Heinlein once titled, a "stranger in a strange land," and my brain hurts, but not quite as hard as my heart lusts.

It's a very odd combination.

But one that lets me navigate my week without too much insanity. Okay, I lie. I am loonier than a tune, but I have learned I have a talent for flirting via text a.k.a. sexting. So that's something.

Not enough, but something.

And given both our schedules, it will have to do. Unless, perhaps, maybe, the universe has a gift in store …

EIGHT

Ah la vache! The white stuff falleth! *Qui cherche trouve!*

Yes, we are, or at least I am although I think that's a bit egotistical even for me, the beneficiaries of amazing good fortune. A circumstance completely and totally unpredicted by all those highly paid weather people, an event, nay my friends, a miracle, better known as Snowpocalypse.

Although I shall tell you Jimmy prefers Snowzilla. He thinks I should, too, because *Godzilla* is the portmanteau, the word merge, from which Snowzilla was birthed. And *Godzilla* has that entire New York City moment.

And no, we are not confusing it with *King Kong* and the ape on the Empire State Building. We do know better than that.

He's referring to the *Godzilla* series opening credits. Jimmy loves *Godzilla*. He still has the TOHO Vintage Godzilla Empire State Building Coin Bank that his great-grandmother gave him. It's the Empire State Building with a huge Godzilla planted to the right side and in front of it. You put in a coin and Godzilla swings about and lights up and monster noises emit. Even I must concede it really is kind of cool. Maybe even borderline geektastic.

Okay, this time I do digress! I know! Hey, come on, you know you've missed that.

Or not. But that's okay. It's so much easier to stop myself when the topic is Jimmy's coolness.

Hey, come on, that's funny.

Or not. Sheesh. So back to Snowpocalypse vs. Snowzilla. I concede Jimmy has a fairly sound argument, but I just don't think Snowzilla sounds as aesthetically cool as Snowpocalypse does. The pop of the "p" is just more satiating than the zilla.

We agree to disagree.

But zero disagreement, this event is more than a weather phenomenon. This, my friends, is a personal gift from the universe. A boon. A bonanza. With the entire city blanketed by huge drifts of snow, everyone's school is shut down, meaning Ava can come out and play too. It's time for Snowball War!

Pings are now circulating madly. I verify the train line is still running and ping Ava to meet me at the statue of Balto in Central Park.

Balto, you may or may not recall, is the sled dog who saved a bunch of children in Nome, Alaska, in 1925 by leading a sled for the final fifty-three miles of the 674-mile trek that started in Anchorage through blinding blizzards and temperatures of minus forty to deliver life-saving medicine.

It's an incredible story. I mean Balto is an example of dog bravery at its best. And I salute him.

However, to be honest, in a world filled with amazing feats, I'm still not sure I get why everyone was so enchanted by this particular Siberian husky that the people of New York donated money so the city of New York could commission sculptor Frederick George Richard Roth to make him a bronze statue. But they were, and he did. At least Roth was from Brooklyn, so I guess that's something. And he did do an amazing job.

You will find Balto standing guard near the entrance to the Central Park Children's Zoo, and when you're little I have to say there's really something about having a watchdog protector that is kind of comforting.

Although, just to be clear, the comforting Balto is *not* a

replacement for the dog your parents won't let you have, no matter how majestic he may be.

Ergo, which I think we can all agree is a great lead-in word. Ergo I pick Balto for our meetup, because first, virtually all New Yorkers can find it, second, it has easy access off Sixty-Seventh, and third and most critically, if you're going into do snowball battle, a little husky magic is not a bad thing. I have a theory. If you can kiss a Blarney Stone, a little husky nose-to-nose can't hurt.

And now that I'm thinking about it, for that matter, neither can a little Ava. Nose-to-nose. Or perhaps, feel free to pause and share a lascivious eyebrow moment, even a little mouth-to-mouth.

Neither of which exactly happened.

To begin with, my trek to the statue took nearly three-quarters of an hour longer between train delays, snowdrifts, and slip and slides. And I'm still here ahead of Ava, who finally arrives with Joe in tow, and her face hidden by a big, silky, multicolored scarf. This isn't completely disappointing, mostly because I do like Joe. He's infectious to be around. A quality I happen to appreciate.

It does, however, put a damper on my nose-rubbing fantasy.

But not necessarily my hand-holding one! My gloved hand grasps onto Ava's mitten, which is sadly less tactile, but thermostatically necessary, and we set out trudging and shuffling, ducking other snowballers, spinning through flurries, and slowly make our way through the park, over toward our texted destination, the Black Tupelo in the Ramble, where we will join up with Jimmy, Imani, Ari, and Vik. Let our pummeling begin.

Between bouts of packing and throwing, I look up, and there are those green eyes, and I don't know, or care, how many times my distractions result in a cold face pounding. Even the icy white stuff that manages to slide under the coat to slip down my pants can't put a damper on me. As long as I can look at Ava, I am impervious to cold.

It is the best snowball fight ever.

Or at least it is . . . right up until . . . *THE SCREAM.*

Imani's tumbling and I'm running and I see Ava looking at me with something I can't quite define, but I know it's not good, and there's no time to stop and figure it out because Imani's screaming and the cold is bone-chilling and I need to save her.

Now!

NINE

She's fine. More or less.

Rolling down a hill in Central Park isn't as dramatic as losing one's footing in the Alps would be. It's more of a tumble down a slope, and while I suppose a person could still break a leg or some such thing, today there's feet of snow for padding and buffeting purposes. But none of that logic applies to we who are the panicked.

Jimmy and I are maybe the sixth or seventh person down the hill, getting there in time to have Jimmy race to help her up. She's pointing and we realize the scream wasn't about the fall. It's about the hand she landed on when she stopped.

Of course, Imani didn't realize it was a hand at first. When she landed, she kind of felt something beneath her. It was covered in snow, but sticking at her in a most uncomfortable way. So she reached down to pull on what she thought was a stick or something to move it away from her tush; only it wasn't a stick and whatever it was, it was, in her mind, reaching up and grabbing on, and that, well that is what launched the scream heard up the hill.

So now, at least a dozen of us are standing gaping at what are now uncovered, skeletal fingers.

Staring down, it occurs to me that if Imani hadn't literally landed on them dead-on, pun only slightly intended, they wouldn't even be noticeable. But she did, and they are.

I bend down and look at the fingers protruding ever so slightly from the snow. And you know, it is really creepy.

I don't pause, hesitate, or honestly even think. I just open my coat, take out my phone from the inside pocket designed to keep it questionably warm and reasonably dry, pull off my soaking wet glove, snap a photo and text it to Detective Robert Tsarnowsky's a.k.a. Tsarno's mobile.

I follow it with a quick message. Dead body. Central Park. Black Tupelo in Ramble. Then I hit send.

And wait.

Which gives me time to turn back to find Ava, who, I confirm with a glance about, never came down the hill, and who . . . my thoughts trail off. The end of my thought just reared an unexpectedly ugly head. True confession, I was about to complete that sentence with "who . . . I did kind of forget about in all the excitement."

Wowzerhole. Cringeworthy am I.

Although I don't really understand why Ava didn't just come down. Imani could have actually been hurt, and granted she's not Imani's bestie, but she is kind of a bestie once removed, and it's not every day someone you know lands on a skeleton poking out from under the ground.

And even if wasn't Imani. I mean it could have been a perfect stranger; wouldn't she want to know?

Well, standing here freezing will not provide answers.

And given the tromped-over, slushed-out area, if there had been a crime scene to protect, it's probably way too late and not my responsibility, so I should just get myself moving back up the hill and go find Ava.

A more intuitive, insightful, or even self-aware person might have wondered about my hesitation. I am none of the above.

I motion to the gang and set off, only to find between the bodies that slid and skidded down and the sun having come out that the trek is now a footslog, which means I am now fighting to keep my boots on my feet and out of the slushy muck with every step.

A trudge here and a plod there finally gets me ungracefully back up, where I don't see Ava. But I do see the first responding police car, which is annoyingly not Tsarno's.

Of course, if Tsarno were first to respond, it would be really odd as Central Park has its own precinct dedicated solely to all 843 acres. It might even be the nicest precinct building in the city, because it's kind of new'ish, or really oldish newish. And the precinct is pretty famous. It's the oldest one in the city. It was established in 1936 from what were the park's original horse stables. But then, which is why everyone knows all about it, they gave it this amazing remodel, just a few years ago.

Yeah, I know. Mini-digress. But only in my mind. My eyes are still scanning for Ava.

And even if Tsarno were here, it wouldn't matter for two reasons. One, Central Park isn't in his jurisdiction, and two, I'm betting the not-very-nice patrol officer in charge, the now-staring-at-me Officer Jennings, would not care to share.

I am using not-very-nice as a derogatory understatement. Dude is an asshole.

Although, in all fairness, before he can ask us any questions and get a handle on the events, he had to call in backup to round up—and out—the thousand or so snowballing teenagers who have zero interest in this latest turn of events.

I don't think he's really having a very good day himself.

But his mood is not my problem. My problem is a missing Ava. And he is not interested in being part of the solution, which is making him my problem, because he wants me to "wait here" and that isn't going to happen right this second.

Before I dig myself a huge hole by informing said officer of such, I catch sight of Joe frantically waving at me. Once he sees he has my attention, he signs, "Ava. Home. Later."

I nod and watch as he heads back down the hill. Only then do I realize I don't know if he means Ava went home and text her later, or Ava went home and, well, later.

56

New tack. I glance about. No Officer Jennings in sight, so I pull out my phone and shoot a quick text to Ava: "with police will come find you at home as soon as i can. xo."

Which turns out not to be overly soon at all. The six of us are still strewn about when the ambulance comes.

Sorry. No. I'm a little distracted here. The ambulance was not for Imani, she's fine. It's an ambulance for the skeletal hand, which it turns out, is attached to a skeletal body.

So, I'm finding this whole thing really weird. I mean it doesn't take a rocket scientist to know we have a dead body. And not even a freshly dead body. Truly we have a very dead skeleton. So, you wouldn't think an ambulance is really all that necessary, but apparently it is.

The way it works is the patrol guys come out when you call. They see it really is pretty much a dead body as advertised, so they set about roping off the area, etc. and call their supervisor. It's the supervisor who then calls EMS, who come out and formally pronounce the body dead and give the time.

While all this is happening, the patrol officers have made their way through about forty or fifty of us, taking down names and contact info.

This, in turn, has left enough time for the squad detectives to get here, and by the time we're finished with our info dump, a new car pulls up. A man and a woman get out, and are greeted by one of the squad detectives.

We all watch intently as they greet each other.

"Crime scene unit," Joe informs us.

We all turn to look at him, but Jimmy gets the question out, "How exactly do you know?"

Joe looks at our faces and laughs. "I forget sometimes when I meet new people they don't know, but I'm pretty good at that whole lip-read thing—pretty excellent as a matter of fact. It's like my superpower. I like to think of it as deaf boy self-defense."

Pause for a smirk and a crossing of his index fingers,

which then spread apart, while his eyes kind of do this slightly buggy thing, "But," he makes an exasperated face, "since some people talk with their hands in front of their mouth or mumble a lot or they turn to talk to someone on their other side, it's an unreliable option." Joes shrugs, and right before any of us react, he continues, bursting out smiling. "But when it works, it's pretty fun."

Something about his smile jogs a brain cell to life, and I grab my phone, shooting a picture of the tableau to text Ava, you know, keeping her looped in, letting her know the crime scene unit is here, good girlfriend moment. However, lest we forget it is freezing out here, I am not as quick as usual, and before I hit send my jacket is being tugged. By Vik. Who is also giving me a head bob right.

I see our gang casually stepping farther away and realize they are on the move sort of downslope, just below the eye-line of the patrol officer who is now eyeballing us. Or me. Good intentions vanish. Text unsent. Joining Vik, doing the creep away.

Which is how we came to be hunkering down in the rustic shelter, the oldest original existing structure in the park or as I like to say, this shelter's so old, it's got no heat. A condition most likely caused by its lack of walls. The Ramble's rustic shelter is basically a roof over old wooden posts, with benches lining the sides, running from, hello (!), pillar to post.

Yes. I know. Not exactly an accurate idiom considering we are now cramming ourselves onto one such bench in a pathetic attempt to generate body heat by having us shiver one into the other, but at least not literally freeze, while the sun lowers, its glare harshly visible from our seats. But it is a feeble attempt at some humor despite my brain cells' impending frostbite.

"Do you people just have an affinity for dead bodies?" Tsarno steps into the middle of our shelter, thankfully blocking the glare for just a moment, while looking rather amused at our crammed presence.

His arrival brings a jolt of instantly warming energy, resulting in highly animated bringing Tsarno up to speed on everything.

At least everything we know. Which I think is pretty impressive considering no one will actually tell us anything.

He grunts a bit. Doesn't say much. Also, doesn't move to do anything with, well, anything. He does, however, take a seat on the bench across from the one he found us on.

So, we go back to just sitting, instantly chilling back down. Imani looks over at me, then so does Jimmy, and so on, as though somehow *I* am supposed to know what to do with the hulky, bulky shadow being cast by the thrust-out legs occupying way too much space, the cat who ate a canary, Tsarno the Barno.

Now, I gotta be honest here. The sun is sinking rapidly. We're all getting colder, exponentially. I was hoping for a bit more information, or something. Not that I know what a bit more would look like, but a bit more. And you know, I know he has it, he's just not giving it up. And that, that wee bit of I-know-something-you-don't-know, is giving him pleasure. "Revenge is a dish best served cold" does cross my mind.

If I wasn't so cold and miserable, I'd be rising to this occasion, but instead I slink deeper into my coat. In my mind, however, I'm taking notes for future opportunities.

"Robert?"

The voice behind the question comes into view. It belongs to a very tall, I mean maybe six-foot-five, maybe even six-foot-six, African American woman. As in we're talking serious presence here. Which is kind of awesome, because I just learned "a bit more" comes in size statuesque and imposing. I kind of like that.

"Reese said you were here, asking for me?"

59

Although her question was for "Robert," her eyeballs are firmly, curiously, assessing all of us.

"Vonnie." Tsarno rises, shakes her hand, his shadow width dwarfed by her height. "Thanks for coming and finding us. Kids, this is Yvonne Nicolls, medicolegal death investigator from the Office of Chief Medical Examiner of New York City. Her job is to investigate any death that falls under the jurisdiction of the medical examiner, including all suspicious, violent, unexplained and, what I think we can assume is most pertinent here, unexpected deaths."

"Now Vonnie, this," Tsarno did one of those open-palm hand motion things at us, "this would be the group of kids who found the body. They would also be the same group of kids who were at the New York Public Library."

Tsarno face twists, doing some kind of oversized, contorted thing, as though searching for a big word, followed by a small faux cough. "Helping," he exaggerates the word, "helping us with that LARP costume thing that night. You remember, body encased in plaster, a certain broken pelvis."

I refuse to make eye contact, keeping my focus firmly on Yvonne, who isn't looking impressed. Nor is she looking happy. The terse line of her mouth is a giveaway. She looks at him, then us, then him, then chews her lip for a minute until finally, "Once I have something I can share on the bodies I'll be happy to."

"Bodies?" I am all ears and questions.

Yvonne glances toward Barno with a look I am guessing is pretty pure annoyance. Although personally I prefer to think of it as askance. But either way it begs the question, is it directed at me for asking? Or at herself for leaving that small door the tiniest bit ajar?

I have never met a small door ajar I don't love to burst open. Just sayin'.

Pause for their silent communication moment to go down.

Whatever Yvonne reads in Tsarno's face is deemed acceptable as she turns back to us, gives a shrug. "I guess it doesn't matter much. It'll be in all the morning papers. Actually, I'm pretty damn sure it will be all over social media long before that."

It will be all over social media? The cue for all of us to turn ultrahip and "lean in."

Her head shakes slightly, the frustration apparent. "The body you found was unfortunately only the proverbial tip of an iceberg. Or in this case, the top of a stack. What you unearthed is some type of mass grave, possibly even a burial ground. We won't know until the historical people get their archeologist out here."

I will report I was cool enough not to jump up and high five. But I will cop to, yes that was an intentional play on words, squeezing Imani's hand.

TEN

So, if this were a TV show, we'd cut away from my reaction, go to a commercial, and come back to something incredibly exciting. You know a *Holy Gadzooks, Batwoman* moment. Of course, if this were a TV show, I'd also be standing here impervious to the cold and looking like Ruby Rose.

Only life isn't a TV show, and as it turns out mine is more of a Dickensian novel than anything else. And no, I do not think I am exaggerating. I'm talking about *A Tale of Two Cities*: *It was the best of times, it was the worst of times, it was the age of wisdom, it was the age of foolishness, it was the epoch of belief, it was the epoch of incredulity*, which is such an awesome line. I mean think about it, the epoch of incredulity.

Until you're living it, then it's a little less awesome. Trust me on this one.

Prior to my tonight, I always imagined best and worst of times as separate pieces of information. You know, the best of times goes in Column A, and the worst of times in Column B. It never occurred to me they could actually be their own double helix.

And today should have been all Column A. I mean it's kind of amazing. Yvonne was right. It was all over the news. And it was our body. Well, it was Imani's body, but that was close enough. We were in the game.

Already there are bunches of Jack the Ripper theories turning up all over reddit and other sites, but the odds-on favorite still seems to be that the bodies, which range from four to, I think, sixteen, might have been part of some place called Seneca Village, which I'd never heard of. Before I deep dive, Imani pings a list of maybe a dozen articles linking to said village.

Nothing like landing on a skeleton to get a person motivated.

I know. That's a bit snarky. But normally I'm the first one off the mark. And the truth is I'm slow because even though we're all in the game, I'm not . . . in the game.

Ava isn't answering any of my texts.

And not just *my* texts. I did think to look, and yes, Imani did copy Ava and Joe when she sent out the Seneca Village stuff. First of all, they were there, and second, I'm sure Imani figured I'd already brought Ava up to speed, so this vast array of intel would make sense. Which is a perfectly fair assumption on Imani's part.

Even if it's wrong.

I knew for certain this wasn't going to be good as soon as I muscled my way down into the snow-delayed, over-crowded subway, pulled out my phone, unlocked the password, and found myself staring at my written, but never sent, text from before, I don't know when, maybe five hours ago. And even that theoretical bring-her-up-to-speed text probably wouldn't have been drafted until at least an hour after Ava left the park.

So we are now more or less six hours further into our day, and she hasn't texted me once. Or communicated on any other platform. There is not a single notice from any app at all.

Forget "not good"; this is just bad.

And ugly. And brings on a severe case of the chronic cringe. That flash of self-awareness, when you realize you've done something so cringe inducing that the cringe twists into a loop, which you can't stop replaying in your brain.

I immediately send pic with a note 'splainin' very quickly that Tsarno had finally made it, we had some news, subways are a mess, so heading home, but will bring you up to speed as soon as I get there.

Which might not be until forever. Because the trains are late and the subway is mobbed, so it takes three trains and everything I have to elbow my way into a car, where I get to stand crushed by New York's humanity for the next several stops. Typing is not an option. Refresh is not an option. Let's see, optimism? You want some optimism? At least it's winter so the smell isn't horrible and the coats help keep gropers at bay. How's that for optimism?

Doors open. I exit. I fight through the sea of humanity pushing into the stairwell, get sideways, and find a wall. Take out phone. Hit refresh. Nothing. I turn off the phone. Reboot. Still nothing. Another train pulls in. Before its doors open, and its masses descend, I race for the stairwell.

Just as I'm exiting, there's a ping. I rush back in, pull off my gloves, and pull out my phone. It's Ari. Our body is on the news.

I shove my phone back into its pocket and rush out into the night.

I slip-slide my way home, sadly getting slushed over by passing cars twice, and as much as I don't want to I do pause, pulling off my boots to text and bring the fam up to speed. Although as soon as I have the boots off my feet, I plead the need to pee, rush to the bathroom, and quick text Ava: "home now. cornered by mom. more in a few."

More silence.

At least from Ava. Dad and my brother, Jean, on the other hand, form a very appreciative audience, making all the right noises, as I rush through the events, talking a mile a minute, my knee bouncing as fast as my mile-an-hour words pour out.

I hit all the highlights in record time, mention it's already made the online editions of all the New York papers, which (thank you, gang) I promise to forward directly to them.

I give a fake smile, flash two thumbs up, rise to leave. As I turn, I hear it.

"Sidonie," she calls out to me, forcing me to wait for her to catch up. "Two things. One, dinner will be in another fifteen minutes or so. And two," her hand now having caught up to me tucks my hair back behind my ear, "you seem a bit . . . *agité?*"

I hate how she does that. Leaves the end dangling for me.

"It's fine, Mom. Fine. Fifteen? Great."

And I escape to my room. Boot up. And start pleading. And waiting. And then my eyes look to my messages, reading. And pause for another round of pleading. And then back to reading.

Hey, I might as well use my ignored time for something. I run through all the papers, and Imani's right. Seneca Village seems to be everyone's top choice. Well, not Seneca Village, exactly, but the section of New York City formerly known as Seneca Village.

Turns out somewhere in the mid-1800s, New York City decided it needed a park. So in 1851 New York City Mayor Ambrose Kingsland agreed to make one. By 1854, the city chose the center of Manhattan between what is now Fifty-Ninth and 106th streets, and construction began.

And what could possibly go wrong? I mean, who could object? It's going to be a park! For the people!

Of course, some of "the people" happened to be living there already, in this very same stretch of Manhattan, and some of "those people," according to a New York state census, approximately 264 of them, were residents of an area known as Seneca Village.

Seneca Village was founded in 1825 or a couple of decades earlier when John Whitehead, a white farmer, sold a young free black man, Andrew Williams, three lots for $125. The same day, African Methodist Episcopal Zion Church trustee Epiphany Davis bought twelve lots for $578.

The AME bought six additional lots the same week, and by 1832 at least 24 lots had been sold to African Americans.

So about two-thirds of the population of this new village was African American, the rest mainly Irish, some German, and even a few Native Americans. There were three churches and a school. And even though about half the residents actually owned the land they lived on, when the government took it, the media of the time described this population as "squatters" and referred to the settlement as "n***er village."

Wowzerhole.

I don't even know how I process this.

A knock interrupts my shock. Before I can answer, the door opens and there's Mama carrying a plate. She looks at me, glances to the screen, and smiles gently, "Your father and brother have *le même visage,* the same face. I think you will all be happy eating with your thoughts tonight."

And as she places the plate next to me, she leans over, ruffles my hair, and kisses the top of my head. "But perhaps your thoughts are even more complicated, no?"

She doesn't wait for me to answer, just turns to leave. At the door she glances back, pauses to say something, or maybe pausing to see if I will, but either way decides no. Instead she gives me another smile, then turns, pulling the door shut behind her.

I take advantage of the interruption to send another text, confused. "i don't understand what i did so wrong. please talk to me."

Again I wait. Nothing. But at least there's more Seneca Village.

So, the government comes in and seizes their land under the law of eminent domain, through which they, the government, can take private land for public purposes. The Seneca peeps take it to court, fighting against both the seizure and the joke of a price they were given, but you know, it turns out even then when the media labeled people squatters and worse, it's pretty much a given that their odds of winning this battle were slim to none.

And just like that, what may have been "Manhattan's first prominent community of African American property owners," as a plaque now built in their honor notes, was gone.

Just gone. And my heart hurts so bad. Filled with pain for them, the people of Seneca Village. Filled with fear for me and Ava and what her silence says. And now I'm shivering, too chilled to answer all the texts flying between our gang, texts no longer giddy with discovery, but now shocked, appalled, and stung by what we have learned.

Somewhere around three o'clock in the morning, I hear the ping. Ava finally answers my litany of pleas and agrees to FaceTime.

As relieved as I am, I'm equally wary—partly because I'm scared and partly because I'm way beyond tired and emotional, which will make keeping up with her twice as hard.

And I am right to be wary. There is no smile, no gentle coaxing. Can we say iceberg. And anything I am thinking to say is caught in the freeze. Frozen solid until her ice queen self-shatters as she hurls the first sign at me. Now she is burning hot, filled with anger.

And her hands point to herself, and then fling forward, at the camera, four fingers hurtling straight at the aperture, growing so big, so fast, I instinctively pull back with some small fear that they will somehow come crashing through and collide with my face.

Before I even adjust, the hand turns and a single finger points back to herself.

It takes me a good minute, even with Ava's face providing an expressively adamant, strident, contextual clue. It's a full-on accusation. "You left me."

Which first takes me time to translate. And then takes time to understand. But then, then I get it.

My hands stumble about, trying to form words. I sign

something along the lines of "I'm sorry. I didn't know. I wasn't," pause to think how to say, "leaving you." Or maybe it should be I wasn't thinking.

This is excruciating. It's incredibly hard to suddenly think in pictures or phrases when words have been my safety net, my defense, my offense for, well, forever. Add to that my emotional state and the sense that something very primal is on the line, and my sign vocabulary is woefully, glaringly not ready for prime time.

I hope my face looks desperate'ish as I spell "Imani" and then palms up, fingers shaped like an "I" facing away, cycle the hands, "screamed."

I follow that by spreading my hands out and pulling a face I hope conveys, "what else could I have done?"

Ava stares at me for three or four seconds, which is a freaking eternity when one is under withering scrutiny. Finally, I get a curt nod. But then come more words, fast, furious, flying at me with no sympathy. I can keep up or not.

"I should be your first thought. What if Imani was screaming because there was danger? A shooter or something? I can't hear. And you, you didn't think about me."

And as I struggle to translate, understand, and ponder their meaning, I see Ava is watching. And as soon as she senses I am caught up, she goes for the kill, "If I can't trust you to be my ears, why do I need you?"

ELEVEN

According to Ari, first fights are very good things. Normal people aren't always lovey-dovey and perfectly thoughtful. Normal people have fights. It's what they do. And, because Ava and I were obviously not dating the first two times Ava sent me away, those don't count as disagreements, never mind fights. So there you have it. Welcome to the world of normal.

I'm not sure I exactly agree with her logic. Although she's right they weren't fights, but still.

However, Vik and Imani are vigorously nodding their agreement, and Jimmy is suddenly stretching his arms wide, cricking his neck in Ari's direction while making bug eyes. Even in my addled state, I get the just-agree-with-her message-so-we-can-be-done loud and clear, so now I am nodding along with Ari's pearls of wisdom, hoping she will run out soon.

I confess, I never thought I'd be this happy to be back in the soul-sucking, cinderblock, fluorescent lit school cafeteria, dining on chips and mystery meat. And yet I am, wait for it, oddly nourished.

Groaner, I know.

But I am that kind of silly happy. The last few days sucked. There was more snow. The city was completely shut down, I was locked in, and our dead bodies were somewhere, literally "on ice."

And even though Ava and I were back talking, it was very

stilted. I did, you know, think about saying she was still cool, rather chilly actually, but I'm not ready to be that cavalier. Not when it's still touch-and-go.

Messaging friends for help was remarkably unsatisfying. Partly because I didn't know how to tell them what was going on. The thought of telling anyone Ava's pissed off because I ran after Imani made me kind of queasy. And it was only half true. She was mad because I didn't think of her first. But I don't know. I need to be with my peeps and to have my peeps tell me it is going to be all right.

And they do not disappoint.

We all agree my actions were unwitting, that perhaps Ava was overreacting just a bit, but it didn't mean she didn't have valid concerns, and that this is all just another one of those "growth experiences" we all loathe.

I raise my milk. "I'll toast to that."

As we lower our assorted drinks, Imani's black cherry soda remains aloft, no longer toasting, just denoting she is now holding the floor. "We have ten minutes left. Did anybody ever find a real body count?"

And like that we are done with me and back to discussing the dead bodies.

Although there really isn't too much to discuss. There doesn't seem to be any account we can deem "accurate," and there are a lot of accounts. Even foreign papers have picked up the story. Trawling online brings up reports, which vary, on average, from four bodies up to fourteen bodies.

There was one that claimed the grave held nearly a hundred bodies and the city was covering it up, but we all conceded that one was not just a random outlier, but really clickbait.

And with that the last ten minutes of lunch passed by.

"Hey, Sid," Imani rises, slowly grabbing her tray, letting the others clear the space, working the super casual a.k.a. super cas. "So maybe you could give Tsarnowsky a call? See what he can find out for us? You know, if nothing else, he might at least tell us the real body count."

Now I don't know why this makes me instantly defensive. Perhaps because the super cas is too casual, as in she is so casual as to be nearly nonchalant. Maybe, one might think, even rehearsed. As though she's been lying in wait for this perfect, choreographed, moment. And worse, maybe it's not just her. Maybe they have all been clued in to whatever this is.

I feel the slight rise of the hackle. Which is totally unwarranted. I know. I mean, first of all, it's a perfectly fine suggestion. Even, we might agree, a smart one. Even if she has stage directed this moment. And second of all, I have no basis for even thinking this, never mind accusing.

Yet, despite her nuanced perhaps-performance, I'm hearing judgment. As though I am quietly being accused of somehow having been neglectful.

Or, sidebar from my kazoo voice, maybe I'm just feeling a little guilty.

Imani, or really any of them, actually could have called Tsarnowsky. I mean it would have been lacking in couth, but they all do know him.

And I didn't think to call him because, well, because I've had Ava on my mind. Argh. Fluck me, inconvenient random thought interruptus, Ava on my mind hops, skips, and jumps right to *Annie on My Mind*, a book I read for my Summer Fifty in the eighth grade. It's about two seventeen-year old New York City girls who fall in love. I think it has a happy ending. I think.

And refocus. Because while I'm busy having a bout of inconvenient random thoughts and trying to recall its potentially happy ending, the present is getting rapidly iffy. Imani's still standing here. Staring at me. Waiting. For an answer. Duck a Flying Fluck!

"Tsarnowsky. Absolutely. Great idea."

I force a smile, grab my tray, and as we head out add, "Maybe we shouldn't call. Maybe we should head over after school. If we trap him, we better our odds."

I feel the cloud of disappointment lift.

Imani shakes her head no. "I can't." But her face breaks into a big smile, totally at odds with her words.

"It's the senior musical auditions. Maybe you and Jimmy?"

I nod, shoot Jimmy a quick text before we split up, heading off to our next class. And at first glance, there is nothing remarkable about this moment.

But this my friends is the exact moment I open the door to my funambulist existence. Funambulism is a funny thing. It has two definitions, the first one being the simple tightrope walking. The second one being a show, especially of mental agility. Together they perfectly describe my sudden turn of events.

Jimmy pings back immediately. He cannot make it today either. Which really shouldn't be a big deal. I can check with Ari or Vik, or I can just head over by myself. And with two minutes before the door closes and science class begins, as I am debating my options, Ava pings.

And it never occurred to me in that moment to say no. So, I didn't.

Not with my first thought. Not with my second. Didn't think about a thing.

Not until my post-Ava, making way back to the train station . . . and my phone pings. Which I don't stop and answer because I'm too busy trying to navigate the street, still filled with huge patches of ice that are way harder to see in the dark, and bonus, it's cold, freezing cold. So, all my FOMO will have to chill with the rest of me. I am not pausing to fish the phone out.

Nearly there, I finally join the overcoated sea of humanity making their way down into the subway, which is still running erratically, causing the bodies to pile up. With the heat pumping in, we are all now trapped in a sauna. Thus, I unzip, and therefore I remember my phone.

The ping was Imani on a group text, wondering how it all went.

How. It. All. Went.

As in Tsarno. The Barno. After school. Today. Like I promised.

Panic. A *can't breathe, full-blown moment of panic.* The phone in my hand is suddenly an alien species and I want to drop it and run screaming up the steps and back out into the dark.

But I don't. I take a deep breath and make a coward's choice, and do something I have never done.

"u—unavailable jimmy-unavailable texted tsarno told him coming tomorrow to see him waiting to hear."

And I hit the send button before I can stop myself. I hear the "zip" of it sending. Take a deep breath and text Tsarno. Tell him we are going to come by tomorrow after school.

The train finally pulls in. I let the crowd push me in through the doors and down the aisle. And with my face pushed against someone's backpack I tell myself it wasn't really a lie, it was just taking a bunch of individual truths and clumping them together for a better narrative—which is not the same as lying.

Of course, it's not exactly the same as truthing, either.

Which is why, when the text from Tsarno comes saying tomorrow he will be in court, but can probably be around the next day, I don't hit the forward button to let everyone know. Nope. Even with my stomach-churning guilt I understand my original text will be on there too, and if anyone thinks to look, they will realize I didn't ask him until way later. And this would be ugly.

But I'm breathing and I'm thinking it's okay; actually it's all pretty good. I get home and send everyone, including Ava and Joe, a note saying Tsarno can't do tomorrow, but he's good for Wednesday.

Imani's good. Jimmy's good. Ari's good. Vik is out. Joe thinks he can get there.

And then there's one more ping. It's Ava.

"thought we were shopping on wednesday picking out a tie for saturday party."

I stare at the message. And for a minute I'm confused. Shopping? Tie? I don't need a tie. But from the other side of my brain there's an answer, a memory, scraffling like a New York City cockroach on speed, carrying a message I know and don't want to hear. Delivering it so loud it's as if she is standing next to me: "*if I can't trust you to be my ears, why do I need you?*"

And I know I'm being played, and that it's some kind of test, but I don't know what to do. And I don't know who to ask.

Actually, that's not true. I know exactly who to ask, but I'm not sure how to ask. Nope. That's not it either. What I really know is she won't like the question.

But I do it. No. Oh no. Not that night. Not even the next day. Yes, I wait until the morning of, when we are climbing the steps, heading into school, and then I finally ask. *Bon Courage.* Yeah. Not so much.

My casual "hey, Mani, would it be okay" not only fools no one, but goes over way worse than I thought. Four heads swivel, eight eyeballs freeze, looking at me with near identical shock.

Imani looks at me as though she has never seen me before. "Just so I am completely understanding this. You want to drop us and move Tsarno from today to tomorrow, all because you have *shopping* plans with Ava?" And although there is a slight pause, it's only to heighten her disbelief with a flip of her hair and rise of her left palm. "Plans you somehow knew nothing about?"

Everyone's face registers as sharply as if I'd snapped a candid and was looking back at it. An image caught for all time. Imani, center of the photo, her face filled with contempt. Jimmy, over her shoulder, his face a face of puzzlement. Vik. Vik's is embarrassment. Ari, frozen mid-eye roll. And me, I turn my imaginary camera around for a selfie. I am haunted, dripping with shame.

I have never felt this small in my life.

Ari's snort of disgust breaks the freeze. She grabs Vik and leaves. Imani stares one moment longer. And I'm trying to understand the twist of her lip that suddenly happens. I can't tell if it's disgust or pain. I want to drop on the ground and plead with her to understand I didn't know what to do and I'm sorry. But before I can move, she too turns and walks away.

Now there is only me and Jimmy.

His look I get. It's pity. But he doesn't turn and follow Imani. Instead he walks down the two steps between us and wraps me in a hug. And into my ear he whispers, "Really, Sid?"

Then he releases me and walks away, taking the steps two at time. So now there is only me.

I have never felt this alone in my life.

TWELVE

Which leads me to doing something I have, maybe not so shockingly, never done in my life. I ditch school. And I head directly to the station looking to find Detective Robert Tsarnowsky.

Who, the desk sergeant informs me, is not in. So I park myself in the waiting room, which is as unattractive and germ-stricken as I remember, but perhaps because my current mood is scummy I currently feel right at home.

I sit, but my body isn't interested. It won't stop twitching and pulsing. I force the has-a-mind-of-its-own left bouncing knee to still, and the right one takes off unimpeded. I cross both legs beneath me, but the right ankle is unleashed and on the bounce.

Mostly I want to take my fists and pound on the side of my head, thinking if I can do that it will let the pain out.

But I can't. Well, not without attracting attention of the not-so-good kind.

Wowzerhole.

That's it. Wowzerhole. I shall challenge myself to a round of "Expletivities!"

Years ago, like way back in the sixth grade, "Expletivities" was a game Jimmy and I made up, which is really just your basic cursing competition. But we gave it a fancy name, and we had lots of scoring rules. The playing part, however, was incredibly simple. We take turns competing, seeing who could out-curse-word the other—the more unique the word, the more points.

And there was a lot more strategy than you might think. Do you use up a good one early in case the other player knows it, too? Do you start with a cheap one or two just to get those points in your tally?

At the time, it was incredibly amusing and, no surprise here, I was pretty darn good, and not just because I had hip pocket additions like my favorite, *c'est des conneries,* French for this is bullshit. Although I loved that one so much I think I probably said it to punctuate every sentence for at least a good two months. And before you start feeling bad for Jimmy thinking my French was some kind of huge, insurmountable edge, remember that courtesy of his mother he came with a few good Japanese ones to hold his own.

The truth is I just like random words more than most.

As a matter of fact, Expletivities is actually responsible for "wowzerhole" being born, but that's a different story track and I don't wish to get derailed for it right now.

So, brain back on the main track, whether I was better or not, when Imani arrived on the scene with her ability to swear in seven languages, me, Jimmy, and Expletivities were all doomed.

Losing got old, we got older, and the game kind of faded away, but every now and then I still find myself occasionally playing solo. One never does know when a "bejabbers" or "thunderation" will come in handy.

I pass the next two hours or so perched on the bench, viciously engaged in my own battle, working to count every expletive I know so I might rack up my score. But some days bollocks are lacking a certain *je ne sais quoi.* Some days emotionally demand one stick with a basic *merde,* or even better a more direct fuck.

Fuck me. Fuck this day. Fuck. Fuck. Fuck.

"Sid?"

It's Tsarnowsky. His girth is not so much towering over as bulging at me, but it's the same basic effect. Considering he's looking at me rather curiously, I realize I never heard him approach so I don't know how long he has been standing here, which could have been two minutes or twenty seconds, watching my fist hitting the bench like an exclamation point for each swear word I think. And now that my metronomic accompaniment has been turned off, I have to say my fist hurts like hell.

I shake it out. Jump up.

"Great. Great. You're back. That's good." I can feel my mind racing as fast as I am nervously jumping about. I try and stop moving, but my hands are now tattooing a rhythmic beat on my thighs. "I need your help."

He stares at me for just a second longer, then nods. I reach down, grab my backpack, and follow him past the desk sergeant and down the hall.

When I emerge, I wouldn't go so far as to say I'm feeling fine, but I can say I am feeling armed.

I make it back to school in time for lunch where I find them through the crush of bodies. The only good thing I can report is they are all here, and no one is looking any happier than I feel. I take a deep breath, square my shoulders.

I slow, approaching the table cautiously, knowing this is not going to be easy.

"Hey." I feel everyone look up, which in turn makes me feel glaringly exposed, really oversized, even a bit mammoth, but I fight the urge to slink down and sit. "I went and saw Tsarno, and he called Yvonne and confirmed there were, are, eight bodies in the grave."

And with that Vik and Ari rise, grab their trays, and head out. Jimmy rises, leans over, kisses Imani on her forehead, shoots me a look, and then he too makes his exit. Message sent. This is between me and Imani. Message received.

She stares at me, nods. I sit.

"I got the lead." She pauses for just a second. "In the play. We're doing *Man of La Mancha*."

I nod. I maybe shrink. Maybe I am already so shrunken she can't see me get any smaller. I don't know.

I don't say anything. We both already know I forgot all about it. Some kid I don't know bumps into my hunched back, squeezing his way past me. Whoever he is behind me, he begins muttering something about being sorry. I ignore him.

"Also, just to let you know, I had a great time at the TKTS Booth by myself in the freezing cold three weeks ago."

I feel my mouth drop open in protest. Then I close it. Open it. Gaping fish anyone? She's right. The night Ava and I went to DC is the night Imani and I have had a standing date four times a year for the past four years.

Every three months, we get dressed up, get in line as early as we can, and begin making our way through the discount tickets booth jam, scanning the boards, debating the merits of each available show, choosing a backup in case we can't get our first pick, and inching forward until we score our tickets.

It started as her thirteenth birthday gift from me and we had so much fun she did the same for mine, and then it became "our quarterly night celebration." This would have been our fifteenth one.

Guilt collides with shame so fast it is nearly impossible to absorb so that I completely and totally forgot all about it, even having texted Imani to cover for me, when Imani comes in for the kill.

"And, worse, you lied to me."

My lowered head pops right up, a sign I am about to hit my nearly automatic denial button, when I realize she's referring to the first time I blew off calling Tarso. The shame is instantaneous, the guilt pounding through my body, making me physically ill. I think I'm going to vomit. I can't imagine how she knows.

79

Imani, staring at me, snorts, "Oh please. We all know you are the worst liar ever. And with all our years and all our BS I never for a moment thought you would lie. To me."

Imani stands up, grabs her tray.

"Make some decisions, Sid. And then own them."

I don't know how long I stayed in the cafeteria. I do know it is Jean who comes and gets me. My guess is Jimmy sent him. It's a very Jimmy move. He won't come because he has to be loyal to Imani, or maybe just because he's angry too, or disappointed or whatever, but even if he is, he won't just leave me. I suppose it should make me feel good, but right now, it makes me hurt even more.

With Jean's prodding I make it out of school and set about walking aimlessly for a while. I think about going to my refuge on the High Line, but somehow I can't. I feel like it would, I don't know, contaminate it or something, I even think about calling Ze, but ze's still in China, and I'm not sure what I would say. So finally, with nowhere else really to go, I turn for home.

I'll never know if Tsarnowsky was concerned about my visit so he called her, or if Jean called and told her about school, or if she just knew because somehow it seems she always does, but I open the door and Mama is right there, just waiting for me.

As my eyes meet hers, mine fill with tears. I feel them overflowing their pocket and slowly, insistently sliding down my face. The ones I tried to desperately blink back are instead draining through the tear ducts emptying into my nose. My jaw shifts left, my nose runs, and then I'm lost to my grief.

I race into her arms and sob like I haven't since I was little. And all of it—Ava, Imani, the body—comes blubbering out of me, a snot-infested, eye-bloating hot mess of a meltdown.

Afterward, when I can stop crying long enough to breathe, we head upstairs and snuggle on top of my bed, the afternoon light already fading, my head on her shoulder.

Her arms wrap around me, and she begins very quietly, soothingly, talking.

"You know how your father doesn't really speak French? Yes, he likes to pretend he does, and sometimes, maybe I think he even thinks he does, but he does not. But when I came here to New York City with him, I had to learn English, real English, not just Frenglish."

I admit. I do open my swollen eye at that, which Mama catches and answers with a smile and a small laugh.

"*Oui,* sometimes I still struggle with a word or an idiom, and we all have a laugh. But your father, you see, he didn't *have* to learn French. It was not an imperative, not *obligatoire*. And these two things are very different."

Mama suddenly stops talking and I turn toward her. I know that look. It's the one that says this is going to hurt, but it must be done. Echoes of her dropping to one knee and looking the four-year-old me in the eyes. *We must pull the band-aid now, oui?*

"I am saying this to you, Sidonie, because in one sense I understand why Ava wants from you all she does. And I applaud her for that."

I feel the tears escape, seeping from my eyes and rolling down my cheek, but I don't move to wipe them away. Mama can see them too, but she too doesn't move to wipe them away. She just continues talking quietly, purposefully.

"But there is a danger here, too. Sometimes somebody can want from you so much that you forget who you are. And if you forget who you are, then you can no longer possibly be the person they said they loved. No?"

And she leans down, kissing my forehead. My body still shakes as I quietly sob.

"Ah Sidonie, *si tu te sens si mal dans ta peau, tu dois d'abord te demander à qui elle appartient cette peau.* If you feel so uncomfortable in your skin, then you must start by questioning yourself about who this skin belongs to. You must always live in your skin, not someone else's."

After that she holds me, cradling me through the big tears until I finally exhaust myself and drift off to sleep. When I wake up, I'm alone with a blanket draped over me. I feel like I have been run over by a truck. I'm cried out, and everything hurts. Rolling over to look out my window, it's dark, but I have no idea what time it is.

I realize I never did tell Ava I couldn't make it there today. I roll back over, reaching for my phone, and oddly I find I am not surprised there's nothing. No text. No email. No chat of the snap. Nothing. Nothing that says maybe somehow something could have happened to me and she cares. Nothing.

I deserve something.

There's also no Imani, no Jimmy, no Vik, and no Ari.

I roll back over and fall back into a restless, disturbed sleep.

THIRTEEN

It's nearly ten o'clock on a school day, and I might have kept on drooling into my pillow were I not woken up by a ping. Nope. Sadly, it's not from one of the usual suspects, neither old nor new. And I double-check quickly, but not one of them has peeped all night. This ping is Tsarnowsky. He will meet me at the Medical Examiner's Office at four, and introduce me to the forensic anthropologist who currently has the case.

A part of me knows he has done this because he feels so bad about my appearance yesterday, which should leave me mortified, but today I don't care. Today, I am grateful.

I take a deep breath, compose a quick note, and send the information to everyone. I don't wait to see if anyone answers as the choice is now each of theirs to make.

I take a shower, let the water wash the night away, get dressed, and head to find Mom in the kitchen. I give her a kiss and say thanks.

"I love you, Sidonie. *Vous êtes mon coeur.* You are my heart."

"*Je t'aime aussi, Maman.* I love you too."

And with that I head out to school. I might be late, but I am going. I still haven't decided what I'm going to do about Ava, but I have decided I am going to do nothing right now. I'm angrier today than hurt. What if I wasn't there because I had been in some kind of accident and was hurt?

I get there in time for third period and pass the gang in hallways, and classrooms, but no one is saying anything. Not that I expect them to. I can't. It was hard enough for me to send the text. I can't. Well, I just can't.

At the last bell Vik comes up, still not saying anything, but begins walking alongside me. I grab the already pushed open front door from the person in front of us, and we exit, nearly to the moment I see Jimmy and Ari come through the other set of double doors, followed by Imani.

We're all still not talking, but we are walking. Heading to East Twenty-Sixth, home of the New York City Medical Examiner's Office, and we're all together, and that's something.

As we round the corner, my heart leaps. Standing outside waiting is Joe. And I look around, but he shakes his head, "no."

I don't actually know I'm standing here frozen and everyone else is several steps ahead until Imani turns, looks at me, and comes back to grab my hand. She isn't speaking, but I don't care. Right now, her hand is a lifeline, a promise that if I hold on, I can find my way back.

And hand in hand we make our way to the front, eschewing the revolving door in favor of the automatic glass doors, leaving behind the grit and grime of New York for the sterile, open, purified-air lobby of the Office of the Chief Medical Examiner. Goodbye exhaust fumes, hello lab antiseptic.

The lobby desk is set way back, and as we begin to cross there's Tsarno and Yvonne, leaning against a far wall, chatting away. I look at her slightly slouched down, using the wall for a backstop, and remember anew how strikingly tall she is.

As we all get signed in and visitor name tagged they approach, and we follow them around the corner to a standard generic conference room.

"Okay," Yvonne waits while we all grab seats, smiles at us.

I sit on the far side, with Joe one chair closer to Yvonne

and Ari behind me, Vik behind Ari. Imani is across from Joe, Jimmy across from me. Tsarno goes to the far end of the long oval table, an island unto himself.

Yvonne doesn't pull up a chair, choosing to stand at the head of the table.

"You obviously have both persistence and," she glances down toward Tsarnowsky, who grunts, "very loyal friends. We don't normally discuss an investigation with, well, just about anyone. So, it says a lot about the people you are."

Just as she's finishing that thought, the door opens and a short-haired woman, just tall enough not to be stocky, but, as the slightly tight arms of her navy suit show, is rather really built, rushes in. The gold hoop earrings she's wearing seem at odds with the rest of her, particularly the small, but not matching, piercing in her nose.

"And right on cue." Yvonne motions to the newcomer.

"Sorry if I'm late." Her apology is aimed at Yvonne. Then, her annoyance is like a bullet straight at Tsarnowsky. "I assumed we were using the conference room right below my office. You know, the one on First and Thirtieth, as opposed to one, oh, blocks away."

"So," Yvonne interrupts this would-be stare-down, "this would be my colleague, Dr. Lena Lolita Renata de la Cortez. And she is the forensic anthropologist working this case."

Joe has taken a seat to my left, and because Yvonne is distracted her head turns away from us while she makes the introductions, and he can't see. I feel the small nudge.

I attempt to surreptitiously, and quickly, spell Dr. Cortez' name. I fail. By the time I get through Lena Lolita, I have forgotten the rest. I do at least think to spell her title, because I have zero idea what sign that would be.

Dr. de la Cortez however, gives a small acknowledge-ment to us, waving a folder she is carrying, while she steps up to the table. She does not take a seat, but looks around, setting the folder down in front of her, and then patiently waits for me to finish. Which would be very gracious if the quiet pause in action didn't make my fingers feel even fatter. Finished or not, I nod, and she begins.

"Thanks, Vonnie. And so we keep it simple; my friends call me Lolo. Now from what I understand you are interested in the bodies from Central Park."

As she speaks, I immediately deduce two things. She is from the Bronx, and Latinx. Bronx accents, even mixed with Hispanic underpinnings, are very specific. I'd guess Dominican, but that's just a guess. I would need to ask to verify. Of course, I really need to ask to verify any of it, duh, particularly given my current state of deductionitis. I could be totally wrong. I don't think I am, but it could happen.

And because she had no idea I'm experiencing internal natters, Lolo is forging right ahead.

And focusing.

"I think you know there were eight bodies found. Sadly, they were not preserved in any specific manner. So, when human remains or a suspected burial ground are found, I attempt to gather information from, of course, the bones. But I also get information from their recovery and excavation, all so I can try to determine . . ." Lolo raises her left hand and ticks off, thumb first, ". . . who died, how they died, and how long ago they died."

Here Lolo stops and looks around as if she is gauging our interest. Suffice it to say it's high.

"I come to a scene in an attempt to read it, to look for small pieces of evidence in a skeleton the way you might read a friend's text. Did they really mean that? Why didn't they use a happy face? Are they mad?"

She laughs and watches as we all knowingly shift but make no eye contact with each other.

"But our biggest asset, as you probably know is, well," Lolo gestures up and down her body, an accentuation to her thinking, "bones are us. Let me give you an example. Teeth. The stages of growth and development in teeth can let us know if the remains represent a child or adult. Another example is the shape of pelvic bones which can tell us with not perfect, but pretty good, accuracy the sex of the person."

A buzzer goes off at the table, interrupting Lolo's lesson. Tsarno hefts himself up, casting an apologetic glance, and heads for the hallway. I realize Vonnie isn't in the room anymore either. I was so busy hanging on Lolo's every word I have no idea when she exited.

"Now," as the door closes behind him, Lolo continues. "In some cases, we can tell by the shape, or the size, or the density of bones if there might have been disease or trauma. If we find what's called a perimortem injury, which would be bone damage that occurred at or near the time of death, without any evidence of healing, such as an unhealed fracture or a bullet hole, it can reveal, or at least suggest, a cause of death."

Once again we pause for an unsaid 'is everybody with me?' Once again, we all are.

"So, armed with that understanding, let's get to our eight bodies." Lolo grabs a chair and pulls it around so she is now sitting at the head of the table with the chair-back facing us. She glances inside the folder she had brought in earlier and placed on the table. Then, with the contents flat, she toys with the upper flap, obviously thinking. Her decision reached, she lets the flap drop and quietly pushes the folder to her left.

"These are tricky. I can tell you we have five females and three males. That they have numerous unhealed broken bones, indicating the bodies were badly beaten. Most likely they were then thrown into this pit, and then someone covered them with a burlap-type sack and doused them with lye. We also know from various markings on the bones that at one point they were all shackled together."

Whoa. Cue gasp followed by a collective cringe. Shackled. The air is forced out of me as a chill races up my spine. I know because I feel it, that with that one word we all froze, joined together in one large icy, biting, synesthesia event.

Lolo eyes everyone, but continues, matter-of-factly going through her report to us.

"Whoever did this most likely didn't know the soil in that section of the Park is highly acidic. And that kind of acidity in the soil, over time, will render most remains unusable for purposes of DNA testing. So the lye, because it was on top, ironically did less damage here than plain old Mother Nature."

And even though we all asked for this, hearing it, listening to it, is still incredibly hard.

"So," Lolo takes a deep breath, "our bad news is, even after cleaning the bones that are left, because unfortunately not all of the skeletons are intact, and after Dremeling," Lolo catches her tech talk and backtracks. "A Dremel is a type of rotary drill we use to get down to any marrow we can find. So first we clean the bones, and then we Dremel. Here, we went after anything that looked even remotely possible, and seven of our bodies aren't going to give us anything more than maybe some mitochondrial DNA."

We must look as crestfallen as I feel, because Lolo smiles maybe just a bit teasingly.

"However, don't give up hope. We still have our eighth body." Lolo's smile disappears, her tone turning more serious. "Before we go there, I do want to take a minute and give each person their due as best I can. They deserve that and more. They are eight bodies with definite African ancestry. This we know from an analysis of their skulls. For example, a skull from Africa would have eye sockets that are more rectangular in shape than those of a European or an Asian. And that's just one illustration of the measurements we explore in reaching these conclusions."

"Let's start with our three men. They were all adults. I would estimate all three of their ages to be anywhere between thirty and forty. Our five women, however, varied a lot more. In our first woman, the bones are thick, indicating a lot of ossification. So I am, for this moment, estimating woman one to be at least sixty-five, maybe even significantly older. Woman two I would make slightly younger, about fifty. The next two women I am thinking fall into that thirty to forty range. This takes care of seven of our eight."

This time the pause is long. Lolo sits and looks at each of us, her arms propped on the back of her chair, hands clasped at their top, her covered mouth leaning into them. It's as though she is weighing something heavy. She drops her hands back down, leans away, but doesn't get up.

"As I said, if we are going to learn much more than that, it will come from our eighth body. What do we know about her? Not too much yet. We know she is a teenager. She's probably just about your age. Maybe a year or two younger. And we know she had the lead shackle, and . . ." for the first time, emotion plays on Lolo's face, her voice breaking slightly, ". . . it was around her neck."

I hear myself gasp. I hear Imani's sob. Lolo pauses for a moment, for us, for herself, and for this young girl, and when she resumes her voice is a bit quieter, gentler.

"We don't know why the rest were removed and hers was not. I can speculate they wanted the length of chain, that it had value, but I can't really tell you. But," Lolo's voice rises back up, "because of this one neck shackle, we have DNA. Because the metal of that shackle, where the iron laid against her skin, protected her neck bones from the elements, and therefore . . ." Here Lolo pauses and smiles at each one of us. When she continues, her voice is triumphant, ". . . her story is not finished."

FOURTEEN

And that's pretty much it. We thank Lolo for her time. Yvonne reappears, tells us Detective Tsarnowsky has been called away, and ushers us out of the building.

We exit to a dark, frigid, almost night, but we all stand shivering in it for another moment. Somber. Reflective. Pained. Yeah, mostly pained. A few weeks ago, we would have just gone to Platitudes, ordered fries, and took comfort from each other. But tonight I am too fragile to bring it up, and no one else does either.

Instead, we all start walking for the closest subway, Vik peeling off first. Ari and Imani should be next, but Imani stays with Jimmy as Ari ducks down alone.

I feel a tap on my arm. As I turn, I see Joe, moving his closed hands one over the other, the top one in a circular motion, like an old-fashioned grinder. "Coffee?"

Every inch of me wants to cup my hands over my ears and shake my head no, but I don't. Instead I meet his eyes, nod yes, calling out to Imani and Jimmy who are now nearly half a block ahead, "Hey 'Mani, Jimmy, I'm gonna go grab a coffee with Joe."

They turn. Imani says something to Jimmy I can't hear, but definitely isn't a, "we'll come too," as they wave back in acknowledgement.

Plan confirmed, Joe and I hustle up the street. At first, I thought he was quiet walking with us because the meeting was so intense, and even though that is most likely true, I

90

suddenly realize he's not so much introspectively quiet as he is nervous, edgy, his eyes darting, looking desperately for a place for us to go inside and sit, which is naturally, even in the city, suddenly nowhere to be found. We walk block after block, his unease increasing my agitation with every step.

Finally a beacon, and we escape into one of those ubiquitous New York City, open 24/7 bodegas, where there's always something for everyone, hot salad bars, cold salad bars, paninis, snacks, and, most importantly, at least in this one, an upstairs loft space for dining. Joe buys himself a Coke, but I just shake my head. I want whatever this is to be over and done. And then again I don't.

Dread is a very not-so-funny thing.

We get upstairs and find it is mercifully empty.

Taking off scarves, gloves, and coats before I dash down and into the bathroom buys me at least ten more minutes before I have to face the inevitable. But now it's here. Out of ways to delay, we sit on opposite sides of an only slightly grimy four-top tucked in the far corner.

Joe turns, reaching behind him to his coat, fishing out what is now a fairly creased envelope. He sets it on the table and pushes it forward, halfway toward me. Then takes his right hand, closes his fist, places it over his heart, and moves it up and down. I watch his face as he signs. He's sorry, very sorry.

I stare at the envelope as if I touch it, it will burst into flames, or maybe I will. So I just let it stay there, halfway between us, not quite touching the cheap plastic white and gray salt and pepper shakers. I stare at it for maybe two minutes, maybe ten. But finally it's time. I give a big sigh and reach for it. It won't say anything I don't already know.

It's short. All it says is, "I did try, but I can't."

I exhale, complete with raspberry. Pass the paper across the table to Joe. He reads it, gives a nod, and passes it back.

We both sit here, me trying to stare at the note as though somehow my laser beam eyes will cause its disintegration, he playing with the cap from his soda, clearly not sure what to do with this, or me, or both.

"I did try to warn you, she's cray-cray." Joe's voice breaks the silence, a forced half laugh.

But the truth is she's really not.

He signs. It's a sign I don't know. He signs it again slowly, only this time he says it out loud for me. "Identity Politics."

I have to say, not what I was expecting. And I must look confused, because he continues speaking, explaining, "Everyone has some. You have some. Your identity? Female. Lesbian. Jewish." He counts them all off. "And maybe you also have queer as in lgbtq, or eyeglass wearer, or Jean's sister, or Jimmy's friend. Or maybe." He stops talking mid-sentence, running his hands through his hair. Suddenly his hands jump, middle fingers extended, "fuck!"

But it's not anger. He's not mad, at least not at me I don't think. I think he's frustrated at being left here trying to make this all somehow make sense.

"Look," Joe regroups, "you speak French?"

At my wary nod, he continues.

"And you speak English?"

"Yes," wary and then some.

"Good," Joes smiles, extends his hands, "now speak them both at once."

It takes a second for the absurdity of his demand to register. Before I answer, he's continuing.

"In the deaf community we have many identity politics. For example, if you could speak French and English at the same time, you would be amazingly capable of simultaneous communication, or sim-com.

See, most hearing people think, even sometimes demand, deaf people should be able to speak whatever their hearing language is while signing, word for word, at the same time. As though sign language, a language that does have its own grammar and syntax, is somehow not a real-language."

Joe's eyes roll and his hands flail in his favorite exasperation gesture before he continues. "And that's maybe one example. But that example is between hearing and non-hearing, and sometimes the biggest identity fight is the one between hearing deaf and non-hearing deaf."

Joe stops again. He's scowling, and obviously annoyed at himself, clearly still not communicating precisely what he wants. I watch him fidget, glance at me and glance away in that well-established movement better known as the age old "should I tell her, or not" dilemma.

"Ava's parents put her in a school when she was little."

Joe leans in, so I do too, and as he returns to signing, it strikes me how, even then, he "whispers."

"I don't know, maybe four or five. She was not allowed to be who she is. She was not allowed to 'be deaf.' She had to be hearing. No sign. Only lip reading."

Joe's anger as he tells this story is palpable. He pauses and I nod, remembering the story of Alexander Graham Bell and the Oralists. As Joe nods back, he switches to speaking aloud, which I know is to take no chance that what he is going to say will be "unheard." "I don't know when, it might even have taken a couple of years, but she tried to kill herself."

He pauses. Gives time to let that bombshell land.

"She got very lucky." Joe sits back, the need to whisper gone. "The pricey psychiatrist her parents picked told her parents to change."

"So," Joe switches back to signing, "you come along, a hearing person." His face is one of overly dramatic shock. He returns to using his voice, laughing a bit. "I didn't give you two thoughts. But you hung in there. And then Ava . . ."

Joe shakes his head, his signing becoming exaggerated, filled with faux shock, or maybe even real shock, I'm not sure.

". . . queen of deaf people, goddess of sign, went and hung in there, too. I couldn't believe it. She went further than I ever thought she could or would. I just think she can't. Not now. Maybe not ever."

And as I'm digesting all of this, Joe shares one last thing.

"Did Ava ever tell you she can speak?" My look must reflect my shock as he shrugs, continuing, almost apologetically, "better than me, actually."

And now I just want him to go. He doesn't want to, but right now I want to not be with him or anyone. I just sit, staring out blindly, until he finally stands.

From the corner of my eye I see him turn back around. I don't react. He moves on. He's halfway down the stairs when he stops, tossing a sugar packet he's glommed at me. I look over, startled by the packet, but not by the action. I remember the first time Ava did that throw-something-at-me thing. It's called beanbagging and is, so I have learned, a perfectly acceptable way in the deaf community to get a person's attention. And it works; I'm listening.

"Just so you know, I didn't come today so I could bring you that letter. I brought you that letter because I was coming, and I thought it was better to come from . . ." Joe's hand suddenly releases the railing and his index fingers hook in a kind of easy C-shape. One hooks the other, and then they reverse. ". . . friend."

I nod, but he isn't finished. He lingers on the step, something else clearly on his mind.

"And" his right hand travels up to his forehead, thumb touching his temple then moving down to meet his left hand's thumb already extended, leaning inward, a signed accompaniment to his voice. "Remember, it's my body, too."

Now satisfied all his messages have been delivered, he's gone. I stay a little while longer, but I can't think here. It's time to move on. I'd already texted home saying I was with Joe grabbing a bite, so it's not like I have to rush anywhere, which, as I fold the note in half and stick it in my coat pocket, is good. Now I just have to decide where I want to go.

FIFTEEN

Which truly wasn't anywhere I expected to be.

First, it's cold so I decide to head back and find the subway. I quickly get to the Twenty-Third Street F/M subway station, not the one I'm looking for, but the one that is here. And since I'm not sure where I want to go, this seems like a fine idea. And thus, shuffling down the steps to the first landing, I come face to face with the jumbo William Wegman mosaic of his Weimaraner dressed in a yellow coat.

And his eyes capture me. And my mouth pulls off my glove, freeing my hand to run down the dog's nose. And the tile makes it feel wet, as though the mosaic is almost alive.

I scooch myself against the black tile wall on the other side and decide that sitting here, keeping company with this puppy, isn't where I wanted to go, but now it's exactly where I want to be.

I hear the occasional annoyance of commuters as they stumble upon me, but I don't care. I ignore them all.

"Hey."

I didn't hear the voice, but I do see the shadow come over me. I look up. It's Jimmy. I glance past him. No sign of Imani. We both know I checked. He nods and sits down next to me. He hands me half of a now-cold street pretzel.

I take a bite. It's gone cardboard. I take another.

"Did you know," I try to swallow, but it's stuck in my mouth. I ignore it as best I can. "That tears aren't all the same? It's true. Their actual chemical composition is different based on whether or not they're happy tears or tears caused by stress, or grief, or . . ." my voice trembles and I fall silent.

Jimmy wraps me up, pulling his arms tightly around my shoulders. But he doesn't baby me. "You hurt her, Sid."

I nod into his coat. "I know. But I don't know how to fix it."

"Ah, Sid, sometimes your job isn't to fix it. Sometimes it's only to own it."

He gives me a big hug and kisses the top of my head. I suddenly wonder how he knew where to find me. Even I didn't even know where I was going. I'm guessing my confusion is showing because Jimmy starts laughing.

"Come on, Sid. Of course, I know where to find you. You are after all my OG, my Original Girlfriend. Finding you was as simple, or maybe as complicated, as knowing you."

And he walks away, climbing back up the steps. He's laughing and flashing stupid, oversized, wannabe gangsta signs, but I'm not laughing. Even as the dark exit is swallowing him up, another figure is entering. She takes the railing, approaching cautiously, but not angry I don't think. Maybe, more concerned.

She stops as she reaches me, "Hey."

"Hey."

Unlike Jimmy, she doesn't join me on the floor. She sits on one of the bottom steps where she can see me. We sit, trying to gauge what the other one is thinking or waiting for or needing.

I suddenly blurt out an embarrassed confession. "Don't think I have a girlfriend anymore."

If there's one reason why I love Imani so much, and always need her so much, this is it. There's no fake, "I'm sorry." Instead, she looks at me and leans in, like she's going to push down my hair, but she doesn't. She doesn't come close enough for that. "How does that make you feel?"

And in that moment, as I think, I realize the answer maybe isn't what I think it will be or even, honestly, what I think it should be.

"I dunno. Sad. Maybe." And I wince and twitch, and then come clean. "Relieved."

"Relieved?"

"Yeah. I knew Ava was kind of playing me. No, that's not exactly right. It wasn't really playing me—maybe, I don't know, maybe breadcrumbing me, but whatever it was I couldn't seem to stop it. Like I was powerless somehow."

Imani stares at me. I see the hundred questions piling up, but all she does is say "Powerless."

It's half question, half statement, all back to me. I turn the thought over in my head. Sadly, I will have to stick with it. "Yeah."

"Why'd you do it?"

I hear Imani's question, but it's only a faint echo of the one I've been discussing with my new friend Slicker, the dog in the yellow coat.

"I'm not sure. It was like from the first moment I saw her, I was quicksanding. And then, you know, she threw out that challenge to find her. And somewhere in there, I don't really know where, it morphed. It became my own fantasy about us, and then I think I got trapped in it."

Suddenly I scoot closer to Imani, as though her nearness is bringing me clarity.

"It's like there were all these levels, and somehow if I met all the challenges and leveled up all the levels, I would be the worthy one, and I would win the fair maiden's hand and, and, and . . ." I'm stumbling, but I have to finish. "And there would be some grand 'my shero' moment."

And OMG that sounds so incredibly lame I just stop. I can't believe that's what came out of my mouth.

I look at Imani, who's looking at me, kind of like I have, maybe not two heads, but at least a head and a half. Thankfully she is not rolling on the floor, or onto the floor, laughing.

"Shero moment." I cringe, but own it out loud. Once again Imani is trying to maintain her matter-of-factness. Although, this time maybe her face is contorting just a wee bit, but not unkindly. "Hmmmm." She looks at me, her nose wrinkling, "I'm guessing not so much."

"Yeah." I give a big sigh. "Nope. Not so much."

And that confession seems for this brief moment to be enough. But neither of us moves. We sit, knowing there is more to give and to receive.

Finally, quietly, Imani says, "You know Sid, when it was your dead body, *that* was all we heard about, all we talked about, all we ran around town about, all we even LARPed about! Now it was my dead body, and it was somehow less urgent, less valid maybe, or maybe less meaningful."

For just a second I think to protest. Then I think again. She's right. Even if my motives weren't to ignore her dead body, the truth is I ignored everyone, and ultimately everyone includes her dead body.

"And I was so pissed." The narrowed eyes, the slight nod of her head tells me she knew I was going to say something and chose to shut up instead. It's a "tell," one I know well.

"And Jimmy kept saying I should give you some room, that you know Sid, she'll be there when you need her. That maybe I was even being a little jealous of this new girlfriend in your life."

Now there's a thought I had not thunk, and probably never would have. Obviously, my wordless communication is working perfectly.

Imani, well she doesn't quite smile, but I do get maybe a grimace and a small shrug.

"And I had to take a step back and acknowledge that was at least partially true."

I absorb that, but suddenly I realize it's deeper. And I feel a surge of anger. "Let's be real, you didn't like her."

For the first time Imani looks away. It's almost as though my anger pushes her face to the right. But when she turns back to me, her eyes are direct, and her voice is even. "No. I didn't. I felt like she was sucking you in. That she wanted all of you, and I was scared she was going to get it."

I don't answer. I sit there, rocking, thinking, until finally, "You should have trusted me."

Imani's eyebrows fly up. Skeptical would be an understatement. But I am spared any flippant response by a loud, distracting noise. Imani uses the railing to pull herself up and take a look. "Sid?"

As I unfold myself to join her, I realize by the pins and needles shooting through my left leg just how long I had been sitting on it. As I'm trying to shake it out, I see what, or who, she sees. It's an elderly lady with one of those wire shopping carts, trying to pull it up step by step, one difficult tug at a time.

We simply head down. I take the cart as Imani reassures the woman.

"There's no elevator in this station." Her fair-enough complaints follow me up the stairs across the landing, up the next flight, where I set the cart down, keeping one hand firmly on its handle until they can reunite. She finally pulls herself up to the top of the stairs, glares at me, and continues her shrill listicle of Twenty-Third Street Station wrongs. "What do they think old people should do? Walk eight blocks in the ice?"

And with that she grabs her handle and is gone. Her thanks unspoken.

We watch her go, look at each other, eye roll. Then Imani looks at me and opens the door. We're done in here.

The cold air stings, but it also feels good.

Imani suddenly laughs, "I can't believe you, of all people, picked a subway cement floor to hide in. You? The germaphobe."

She's right. Totally. I shrug, "It came with a dog?"

I'm kind of wondering if I should go back to where we were, which I believe was Imani acknowledging she was maybe a little jealous of my new girlfriend, maybe even a bit inappropriate in her behavior, when I feel her firmly loop her arm through mine. And with that Imani is steering the direction of both our feet and our conversation.

"You know, Sid, when I came to America I was terrified. I don't know if I've ever told you this. To state the obvious, at that time I didn't actually know you. And after, when I did know you, I forgot all about it. So anyway, there I was, transferring into the seventh grade, after classes have already started, and after my not so fabulous teenage growth spurt has begun. They have me waiting in the office, they bring you in, and it's like hey, we got you a best friend. Which would have been totally laughable except, on that day, in that meeting, I knew everything suddenly was somehow going to be okay."

I take a chance, turning to her, flashing a big toothy "of course" grin.

"No," Imani shoulder pushes into mine. "Not because you are *sooooo* fabulous. I remember those glasses. They were even sillier than that random thought of us two, instant best friends in the making, was."

She's sadly not wrong.

"It was . . ." Imani slows down, bites her lower lip, thinking. "It was because other than what we saw on television, which when you go to boarding school is limited, I didn't know anything about America. I mean yes, I knew Disneyland and I knew for damn sure who the president was. I am, ahem, three-quarters Kenyan. It doesn't get holier than Barack Obama."

At that Imani tips her head and her hand circles forward in a spiraling flourish.

"So now I'm heading to the home of the *black* president who lives in the *White House*, near the happiest place on Earth, and I think we both know I am knowing nothing real about living in America."

Without breaking stride or the conversation, her shoulder-push signals turn right at the corner.

"But growing up, no matter what country I was in, there was one constant, one very specific show I remember. *Sesame Street.* And of all the American things I didn't know, and therefore was afraid of, I actually knew that long before the Cookie Monster discovered cookies, thereby becoming Cookie Monster, his name was Sid."

Imani stops walking and spins me toward her. "So, I mean, come on, short of maybe having a new friend named Bert or Ernie, what could be a better sign than that?"

I grab her, and wrap her up in a hug.

She whispers in my ear, *"tu me manques."*

It's not soft and gentle. It's low, and it's fierce. In English we'd say I miss you. But in French, the words literally translated become "you are missing from me."

I tighten my arms around her until they cannot be more.

We break apart, and I'm crying because apparently that's all I do these days, and she takes her gloved hand and wipes the tear. And then her tears began welling up, her face growing blotchy. I know she doesn't want to cry, even if I'm the one who started it. Crying is intimate. And I know our relationship hasn't been good enough for that to happen right now, but it might anyway. *Can I trust you now?* The silent question passes between us as though it is being screamed across the street.

"And so here I come, chubby, overbite me, completely clueless about American race. Your politics weren't mine. I was born in Kenya, raised all over the world, sheltered by culture, class, education, and money. Slavery was a terrible thing, but it wasn't really my problem. It was history. And it wasn't my history. It was something in books, something on TV. Only now I realize I was wrong. Slavery is my history."

Imani's fist rises up to her mouth. Her body twists. I watch her struggle to fight back the still-threatening tears and find the clarity she wants.

"You know, Sid, it's like when you talk about the concentration camps. It doesn't matter if those people were your

101

actual grandparents. You only care that they were somebody's grandparents, and they lived and they died and they must be remembered." Her fingers dance in the air, a silent castanet, looking for something, "What's that word you use?"

I don't have to ask which one she means. *"Zachor."* To remember. To never forget.

"Exactly. No one I see on the subway or in the store says to me, "Oh, you're black, but that's okay because you aren't from here." No one says, "Oh, you're black but not African *American.*" And now I get it. I realize it doesn't matter because to them I am black. That's what they see. That's all they see. So, like you, I'm who is here. I have to remember."

For a moment, it's like she's done. Her body sags slightly, as though the weight of her words has caught up and they are too much, too heavy. I move, but her hand comes up quickly to stop me.

"So, no." Imani straightens. "I'm not from here. The irony is that the real truth is so much worse. I'm from Africa." Imani's short laugh is harsh, painful. "I'm *literally* from where she's from. Our dead body? She could be my great aunt, or my cousin, or my cousin's cousin. She could be me. And I, I could be her. And I found her. Or maybe, you know, maybe she found me."

"But either way, now she's my responsibility. I need to know her. And I need us all to know her. I need someone—no, I need me—to say her name. To say she was Liza or Sue or K'teesha or whatever, and that she lived and she died and she wasn't left in some hole somewhere, covered up with dirt, and just forgotten."

"And," Imani gets as close to me as she can. There is no longer anything but she and I.

"I can't do this alone. I need, as you would say, my posse. I need Jimmy and Ari and Vik and . . ." Imani's eyes are boring into mine. "I need you. I need my best friend to help me find her name."

102

"And once I know her name, I'm going to whisper it, speak it, and scream it out loud. She is not going be left lying there, some Jane Doe with an iron neck shackle and a toe tag number on a slab in the morgue."

Imani's intensity is palpable, waiting, pulsing. She is all soul on bone. Whatever tears had once threatened to fall are gone, eaten by the righteousness of her fury. And it is righteous. And noble.

And it is not a schoolgirl's fantasy.

She is not going to be Jane Doe with an iron neck shackle and a toe tag number on a slab in the morgue.

I look up to the sky, making a silent promise. One I don't know how we will keep. One I don't know if we can keep. But I promise Imani and I promise *her*, whoever she is, we will find her. Somehow.

SIXTEEN

Soooo, you're probably thinking I bolted out of bed the next morning, ready to take on the world, to go forth and tackle my mission. Not quite. After 'Mani and I didn't so much as regain our footing, but kind of found new footing, we used it to climb our mountain. Then we went over to Platitudes, where Jimmy had gone ahead to wait.

I'm just gonna say it was a very late night.

Ergo—I did tell you I am loving that word—when the alarm rings, it is way too early because I am still emotionally exhausted. A cranial sinkhole of feeling. A true brain drain. And it's getting worse, not better.

It begins so weirdly it's almost like a "big brother is watching" moment. Here I am, forcing my eyelids to lift, then my body to sit, and here it is, a text waiting for me. It reads: "There's a proud history of solving crimes before we had DNA. You have clues. Follow them."

Tsarnowsky. I toss the phone back down. Exhausted exhale. Someone should tell him no one texts in full sentences. I pick the phone back up and read it again. *You have clues.* It's like he's taunting me, daring me to do this. Which, of course, we all know I am totally planning to do. Even before his text. So why the dare? Weird.

I feel a little exposed, like I've just been, I don't know . . . search-engined. There are reasons I keep my computer camera covered and my privacy options turned on.

However, there is no time to dwell. I have places to go,

promises to keep. Must get to school early so we can organize. I look in the mirror and hair's not great, but it will pass. I grab jeans, and as I'm hopping to pull them up and close, there's a knock on the door.

"Sid?"

I stop hopping and stand there, fly unzipped. Oh no. That is not Mom. This is way worse. It's Dad. "Yes, Dad?"

"May I come in?"

Bad. This is bad. I need to be getting out of Dodge, now. I have no time for this. "Sure."

"Hey! Dad!" I go for light, cheery.

He takes a minute, saying nothing. I'm guessing he's overcome by the vision that my well-appointed outfit of jeans, bare-feet, and slept-in T-shirt creates.

"We missed you at dinner last night, everything okay?"

Oh no. It's a case of the Daditudes. They come in two specific bundles. Bundle A—we're not happy with those grades. Bundle B—we're worried about you.

"Yeah." My hands splay apart, moving back and forth, perhaps just a little bit rapidly. "Fine, actually. I mean it wasn't, but it is. The Ava thing, you know, it was hard, like really hard, but it's okay. Now. I mean it's okay now. Really."

"You're sure?"

"Yeah. I mean Mom was great. And it sucks, but it's all good."

"Okay then." But he's still's not moving; he's still watching me. I give him a hands-wide, double thumbs up.

"You know I love you, Sid."

"I know. I love you, too, Dad."

And that is finally that. He's turning, leaving, and . . . never mind. He turns back, his face serious.

Warning. Danger Sid Rubin.

"And Sid, one more thing. We don't get to come and go as we please in this house. We have courtesies, we have cell phones, and we have curfews. Understood?"

Dad-nabbit. It's the Dad Double Bundle. And he's

requiring me to sign for it. He is not simply turning and going. No, he's standing here, waiting.

"Yes, Dad." Might have been a little meeker than I would like.

But I can't complain. It could have been much worse. As I turn, I spot myself in the mirror above the dresser, which also happens to have a handy dandy clock. And fluck me, time to step it up. Slept-in T-shirt off, new clean T-shirt on, flannel shirt on, hoodie on, coat in hand, and I am outta here.

I try calling our pal Ze on my way, but ze isn't answering. Maybe out to dinner? Of course, I'm assuming Ze is still in Shanghai. I still can't believe Ze went back, but I guess now that they are famous for their role in our game of *Contagion* hostage rescue, zir family is way more chill about what ze says they call their "other gendered" child. I miss Ze, but I am truly happy they are having a happy ending, too.

Anyway, I will text Ze after our meeting.

To which I am first. And that, my friends, is by design. As we know, I have been too neglectful for too long. Today I am going to be front and center. Well, from the sideline. This is not my show. It's Imani's. Not my show. I'm hoping if I say it enough, I will absorb it, and my actions will reflect it instinctively.

Phone buzz interruptus my chant. And I'm looking at the smiling face of Ze. I give a quick glance around, but as far as I can tell the library's still empty.

"Sid! So cool, I was just thinking about you. Last night I go to dinner and a friend uses the expression 直男癌, which in the United States is what is called toxic masculinity. But if you actually translate words from Chinese to English, it is "straight male cancer." So, I am laughing and thinking who do I know who would need to know this? And as I say, but only when I am in Paris, *voilà!* The phone rings. Here you are!"

Wow. There's a lot to unpack here. One, I'm not sure I do need to know this toxic masculinity thing, and two, I'm not even sure it's funny, but whatever? Time is not on my side.

Before I say anything, Ze turns the phone camera and I see Qi grinning away and waving hi. Just as quickly, the phone turns back.

"Hey, Ze, that's great." I turn, smack-dab, right into the waiting-for-me-to-notice-her librarian. Who is actually holding the front desk sign that says *no talking on cell phones*. I give her a two-minute beg sign with a best plead face. I mean, c'mon, there is nobody else here right now.

Ze, of course, is still talking. "So cobots are the future. Makes it more . . ."

"Two minutes."

I nod and just cut Ze's collaborative robot chat off, literally pulling the phone back and waving so they will see the interruption.

"Look, I know I owe you a call and I really do want to hear all about the cobots, but now is not a good time. So, here's the thing. I need you to help me build an app. I'm not sure exactly all it will need, other than it's gotta be done fast. You up for it?"

Confirmed. I hang up.

And cue squeal, which makes me turn around. And almost before I register her, I am wrapped up and nearly suffocated by Ari and her bosom smush. Yes, I am face planted. Wow. I am never copping to having missed that, but I have. Hey, her "girls" are def special. And her hugs are just the best.

"Oh, thank god you're back." And released. "We are so over her I can't begin to tell you."

And fortunately for me, she can't. Because Jimmy and Imani show up, and just as we are snaking our way to a table in the back of the library, Vik catches up.

For a moment we all just sit here, nobody saying anything. Imani finally looks at me with eye-popping exasperation. It's her *"god Sid, you are such a moron"* look.

"All right. Look, Sid." Imani breaks the silence.

Me? I'm honestly not sure what I have done this time to merit being called out.

"You are definitely not sitting here and out-politing me. Not only doesn't it really suit you. Actually, it's kind of laughable."

I must look as stricken as I feel because Imani softens her blow, "Although your politeness is appreciated and somewhat endearing. But we just have no time for it. We have one object, which is to find out who she, our skeleton, is, was, and I'm perfectly happy to say I don't have those kinds of skills. I, I am a total English Theater person, who also happens to be, ahem, the star of the senior musical." Pause to flip hair, run hands down body emphasizing her mini-finale move, strike a pose.

Continuing on, "You, however, are a math, science, annoying need-to-know brainiac of the highest order. Ergo . . ."

I smile even as she pauses to shoot me a smug face. It's her playful smug.

"You need to lead this. But," Imani's left hand raises, index finger extended, "to quote you, 'never leave your wingman.'"

Yes, I know. She's really quoting me quoting Jimmy, quoting *Top Gun*, but it's all good. Her point is made, and taken.

"Hey," Vik moves us on. "What do we think was in the folder Lolo brought? I mean she obviously had it with her for some reason?"

"Photos." I answer. "I'm thinking Lolo brought either autopsy photos or maybe crime scene photos. I don't think she wanted to lay them out in front of us."

His question triggers something else. "You know what I don't know?" Correction. "What we don't know?" Rhetorical. No need to wait. "How old are the bones? She never gave us an age or a range. Nothing."

"And," Ari jumps in, "here's another question. If there is mitochondrial DNA, would that let us know if the three women are related, if all the people are related, at least on the mother's side?"

That stops the conversation in its tracks. To say no one

108

was expecting that particular question to be in Ari's wheel-house would be another rung on the never-ending ladder of understatement. A ladder, for those of you who may not know, is often found leaning on the wall of bitter irony.

"Hey," Ari looks at all of us looking at her and laughs. "My mom is the queen of the murder-of-the-week shows. I will have you know I can speak 'evidence' with the best of them."

Good to know.

I pick up my phone, google the number for the Office of the Medical Examiner, call, put it on speaker, and set it down in the middle of the table. As it rings, I realize I am missing key information. Damn it. I lean over, disconnect.

"Anyone actually remember Lolo's name?"

Everyone laughs, Vik signals he wrote it down. I dial again while he digs his notes out of his bag, finds the page, and turns it around so I can read it. This way, if we ever get through the menu and actually get a live person on the line, I will be ready with a name.

OMG, there's even a prompt for law enforcement if they're calling to report a death. I find that kind of surprising. I just figured they would somehow have a direct dial.

Of course maybe they do. Maybe it's just in case they forgot it.

And success, a live person, "Office of the Medical Examiner, how can I direct your call?"

"Hi. We're trying to reach Dr. Lena Lolita Renata de la Cortez."

"Hold the line while I put you through."

And it's ringing. And we're all waiting. And it's not ringing.

"Hello? Hello?"

We've been cut off.

Which is how Ari and I, after we all sat through this painful phone-go-round another three times, eventually wind up going to find Lolo after school. She is in and agrees to come down to talk to us, although as she steps off the elevator she doesn't seem very happy to see us.

"Okay." She turns from Ari to me, a frown on her face. "I'll tell you what. Ask me your questions, and I will answer them if I think I can without breaching confidences, but only this once. When the DNA results come back, they will belong to the police. That's who will control the flow of information. You will need to go through them."

Once Ari and I nod our understanding, she continues.

"So, we did not run a radiocarbon dating test," her head shakes, but at least she is smiling sympathetically. "If these bones were some type of archeological discovery, going back in history millions of years, along with radiocarbon there are incredible amounts of tests available to run, such as biostratigraphy or paleomagnetism . . ."

Ari has been typing frantically into her phone and looks up helplessly as Lolo finishes her thought, ". . . that help us compare or find order to establish timelines."

Lolo looks at us both and laughs. "The names of the tests don't matter. We're not running those. They won't help us. I can assure you the bones you found don't go back even half a million years."

Ari drops her phone into her bag as Lolo continues.

"So that's one side. Let's call it the million-plus range. For the other side, if you go back just a couple of years, we've got various ways to get pretty accurate readings, many of which have to do with things we might know directly about the victim and the condition of the body. Which leaves us with the particular challenge this case presents— the midrange years. Dating these years gets tough. But, fortunately for us, this is one problem where our . . ."

Here Lolo hesitates, scrunching her nose, motioning her hand, searching for a word.

". . .our expertise weighs in. Once we saw these bones, we knew this grave was well over a hundred years old. Without getting lost in detail, if you view skeletons for a living, the coloration of the bones pretty much tells us that right off the bat. So now we have to look for clues, maybe an artifact, maybe something in the iron content, maybe something in the teeth chemistry."

Lolo pauses again, assessing. I'm beginning to realize this is what she does when she is debating how much to tell, and I try to look reassuring, even though I'm not sure how exactly that looks.

"Look," Lolo exhales loudly, "we don't have all the answers yet, and we may never. I can tell you, had these bodies been discovered in any other way, in virtually any other place, we wouldn't even be this involved. Our rough estimate is we are looking somewhere around the year 1800. This means there is no current grieving family to assuage, there is no criminal prosecution to be made, and the harsh truth is there is no unique or compelling forensic interest, other than as . . ."

Lolo stops again, letting the sentence hang there unfinished. She looks at the two of us, not unkindly, maybe even sympathetically, but then she finishes it, delivering it with a sense of finality. ". . . fodder for headlines."

Both Ari and I go into denial mode, but she raises her "talk to the paw" hand, forestalling an argument.

"As I said, if you want to know who is buried there, the police will have our test results. But you need to understand this isn't an episode of television. We do not have anywhere near enough manpower or budget to go around to even the grieving families who desperately need us. If you want answers, you'll need to somehow find them yourselves."

SEVENTEEN

We stand there watching Lolo turn away.

Then we head out, saying nothing. But I know our quiet isn't any kind of defeat. Nope. Our quiet is only a shared moment knowing we are both hearing Lolo's voice echo, "you will need to find answers."

Our next destination is not our usual Platitudes, but rather back to school, where we are all set to meet up and grab pizza before Imani's rehearsal begins at seven. And it's already past five thirty. Ergo—hey, rule of three—we decide subway will be fastest, even though it will be rush-hour packed.

We're hustling our way down the stairs, left side clambering, and I know you would think I'd be rambling on about Lolo's bomb of an answer and what we're gonna do next, but surprisingly I can't. Ari's earlier comment keeps getting in my way, and not in a good way.

"You know," I say as we push through the turnstiles, "Ava's not a bad person."

Ari looks at me, confused.

"No, she's probably not." It's an agreeably, cautious response. "Seems fine to me."

Now I'm confused. "But this morning you said you are so over her."

Ari gives me an "I did?" look, then suddenly laughs. "Sid, that so had nothing to do with her. It was all about you. When you're with Ava, you're not Sid. It's like Sid goes off and sexiles herself."

We're queuing up for the next train as best we can when our conversation is overrun by increasingly loud clatter. We wait for a non-stopping train to scream past.

Ari uncovers her ears. "Where were we? Right. You were being all deference and stuff. Like some sort of big bad butch . . ." Ari pauses, her nose scrunching, ". . . coquette. And god, it wasn't even mildly amusing. Well, that's not fair. It was, for a while, mildly amusing."

Then, as if coming to her senses, she stresses, "A very short while. So, when I said I'm so over her, I wasn't talking about Ava, I meant it about you, and how now you might go back to being you. I probably should have said, 'thank god because I'm so over you.' Because honestly you need to own this—not her."

I know. It's pretty fugly. But then I drift back to the last time we sat, just the two of us, and talked on the High Line. Ari's not being unkind. She just owns things. And she doesn't pull punches.

The pulling in of the train and the pushing of the crowd saves me from needing to answer, but once I'm aboard I look around until I find Ari's multicolored head three people back. I get just enough movement to lean right and smile my thanks, or maybe just my acknowledgement. I don't think I'm ready for thanks, but I want Ari to know I'm not mad. And I want her to know I kind of get it now.

Ava needs someone I can't be, someone born into her world, because she had to fight so hard to get it now she won't risk having it taken away. And now I get it; that isn't me. Which is kind of okay. But it's not okay that I, of all people, didn't have the words, the language, to tell her I couldn't be that person, the person she needed, before I wasn't.

I somehow stay upright as the train lurches out.

The pizzas, which I can smell as soon as we head down the hallway, are on a table in Mr. Clifton's room with numerous slices already devoured. We dive in and bring everyone up to speed.

"So, no guess?" Vik speaks everyone's question.

I shake my head, slumped deep in a sofa, my mouth filled with pizza. "Nope." I pause and manage to swallow the oversized bite ripped from my folded slice, and even more importantly I catch the grease running off the back end before I am wearing it.

"But we did get the name of the State Historic Preservation Officer a.k.a. the SHPO person, who we can track down tomorrow."

Note to self, way to shut up a room. It's kind of like the anti-mic drop. So we all sit here, literally chewing on that for the next couple of minutes.

"Okay," Imani breaks the silence. "I have ten minutes before rehearsal. Anyone have any ideas?"

"I have two incredibly loose thoughts," I offer. "First, we have to all agree that since the bodies were all . . ." Wow, some things are harder to say out loud than when they were just thoughts.

I gather up my voice, which is currently rebelling. "Since they were all chained together, they had some relationship. We don't know what that relationship actually was, but we know it includes eight people. So, my first loose thought is the library. Well, kind of. My first loose thought is the newspaper. I thought we could start with *The New York Times* archives, but actually *The New York Times* didn't begin publishing until 1851, which puts them outside the window."

And no. I did not know that offhand. I googled.

"But there were papers. Other papers. And even better, in 1801, right in the center of our sweet spot, *the* Alexander Hamilton, of yes, Lin Manuel Miranda fame, founded the *New York Evening Post*, which is now the *New York Post*. Of course, I have no idea if that *Post* looks anything like our *Post*, which we all know loves a screaming headline, but if it did resemble it, it could hold a possible lead."

Hey. One *New York Post*, one Alexander Hamilton, and one Lin Manuel Miranda, Imani's not-so-secret crush, lets me think there's maybe a semblance of a good omen evolving.

I know, as far as those ray-of-hope things go, it's pretty dim. And pause for a cheap chortle. It's sadly pretty much all I've got right now.

"And there were earlier papers, lots of them. So, I'm thinking we head down to the stacks and start checking whatever newspapers we can find for eight missing people or eight murdered people or something with eight."

Suffice it to say, good omen thing or not, there is no applause following this.

"So," Jimmy looks up. "You said you had two loose ideas."

Before I can get started on what I know is an even less spectacular thought, Imani jumps up. "I'm late." She leans over, kisses Jimmy. "Thanks for going, guys." She looks over to me, "I'll get details later?"

I nod.

"I know you got this." And she's gone.

Leaving the four of us to polish off the remaining slices, clean up and, you know, make a plan.

I go back to answering Jimmy. "I don't know exactly. But somehow the census popped into my brain. I'm thinking something to do with the census. But I don't know what. I did check. The first census was in 1790. So it is in our window. And they do it every ten years."

"So, we look at deaths for ten-year periods?" Jimmy's confusion is plain to see.

"Exactly. I just don't know how, or if, it helps. So that's a problem."

And with that we kind of just split up. Vik and Ari leave while Jimmy and I make our way through the halls to the theater. Outside the doors I reach over, stopping him before he pulls them open.

I don't hesitate. I just look directly at him. "Thank you."

He gives me that small big brother grin. The one that says I am exhausting. Sadly, I know it well.

115

"Just happy to have you back."

"Was I really that bad?"

"Yeah. But we all love you, so it's okay."

It's the wink that lets me know he's teasing. I shrug and we both reach for the double doors, opening them as quietly as we can. And the only voice we hear is Imani's, coming from center stage.

We stand there, at the back of the auditorium, hidden in the dark, watching, listening, as Imani pleads with Don Quixote.

For anyone who might not have a Broadway Bound Bestie, here's the short version: old would-be knight Don Quixote de la Mancha sets out with his would-be squire, Sancho, in a quest to restore the age of chivalry, to battle evil, and to right all wrongs. During their quest they come upon a self-described whore, Aldonza, who Don Quixote insists, repeatedly, is his "Lady," Dulcinea. And before the show is over this crazy knight changes everyone's vision of themselves for the better.

As she sings, it's amazing how the words and the music take on new meaning. I feel every note twist in my heart. She's in sweats, flats, hair pulled back, but her face tells me and her voice gives me everything I need.

He's right. She's right. They're right. Cervantes is right. The goose bumps running up and down my arms, the chills running up and down my spine, are right. It is never too late to set out on a quest in order to right a wrong. To sally forth.

And maybe, pause for a hat tip to Miguel Cervantes, you know, we are tilting at windmills, but they are our windmills to till at.

Which is why I race home and spend my next two hours WhatsApp'ing with Ze, tilting and questing away as we build an app to combine the research and the leads in some way to get us to an end goal.

And we shall call our new app Dulcinea.

Yes, go ahead and roll your eyes. I will grant you it might

be a bit cheesy, even maybe more than a bit cheesy, but I think calling it "The Quest" is even cheesier. And we don't have all night to think about what to call it when we need to build it.

In my mind I see one of those big maps they show in the movies where they stick pushpins in and Post-its on, and strings run all over the place.

So, we agree on a map module, but just for Manhattan for now. And we can color-code for hypothesis vs. fact. This way, if we have either definitive information or someone has an idea they want to call attention to, it all begins here. And then we can add more colors as we need them.

While we discuss, Ze is already speed coding, and without looking up nonchalantly says, "Sid, sometimes you think a person can be your person, but that doesn't, and won't, make you hers."

She may not be making eye contact, but I'm staring at the screen, surprised, even though I suppose I shouldn't be. I only know Ze because ze and Imani went to boarding school together in France before Imani moved to the U.S. Imani would def have turned to Ze if I were being a useless friend. Which I was. So I can't begrudge her that, but apparently I can still be pissed.

Because I'm tired, tired of feeling like I'm somehow the punching bag in this equation.

"You know what, Ze, that's for me to find out. It's not for everyone else to determine. Imani has Jimmy, Ari has Vik, and guess what Sid has? Oh yeah, nobody. Sid has nobody. So maybe, in all their coupledom, they could have spared five more minutes of generosity instead of judgement."

And with that a silence falls. I busy myself working on the home screen, which we have decided to do with icons.

"Shit." Ze stops chatting long enough to rewrite an apparently finicky strand of code. Finished, she casually changes subjects, "So, if thieves wear sneakers, and artists wear Skechers . . ."

And I freeze. *Codus Interruptus.* Ze found a meme. It's gonna be a long night. But I answer, because, well, because I can't not answer. It's a pun thang.

"Plumbers wear clogs."

A brief moment as though there is thinking going on, but too brief to actually think. I know now, Ze's been prepping.

"UPS people wear Reeboks."

For a minute I think about it. Then I get it. Like re-box. Wrong spelling. So I'm not sure it should count. Before I decide, Ze interrupts.

"Get it, Sid? Like UPS, like post office. Reeboks."

Ze is way too entertained by zir own pun. So just as I think I should be flagging it, I think again, and let it go. Let's be real, I couldn't play this in Chinese if my life depended on it.

I'm in. "Okay, I've got one. CIA peeps wear Hush Puppies."

"Ooh. Good one." Pause in the game for a moment of business. "I think we use flags for places we've been, but need to find more. You know, like we've flagged this one."

I don't answer as I'm trying to finish this line before I lose track of it. And bracket.

"And Sid," Ze's voice causes me to look over to my screen. "Would it really have changed anything with Ava if everyone was fake nicer about it?"

I stare at zir, thinking about that. Probably not. But that's not what I answer.

"So, I'm good with the flags. But I'm not so good with the analysis. You know, sometimes it sucks being the fifth wheel. It's like a bad version of Duck Duck Goose—Couple Couple Sid. And it was like I finally had someone, and I just think," I pause and then let my anger fly, "they, my so-called friends, needed to be more something."

And I sit here, coding and stewing, angry with them, angry at myself for not being able to articulate my hurt better. More what? I don't know, more supportive, more understanding.

But they were more for a while. Imani came with me to learn sign. Everyone cheered us on during the post-roller derby makeout session.

And suddenly I get it. Regardless of Joe trying, and Imani, and even Ari, I finally get it. Ava was doing what Ava needed to do to take care of Ava. I feel my heart ache, and I feel my head set free, all at once.

"Hey, Ze. Movers wear Vans."

"Traitors wear flip-flops."

"Scholars wear oxfords!"

This continues intermittently for the next few hours. Finally, Ze takes pity and says they would finish the timeline module without me. For which I am truly grateful. But before I go, I have one last meme to play. Hey, it's me and it's a word challenge. Don't judge.

"Funambulists wear New Balance."

The laugh echoes as I disconnect. I'm not sure if it's because Ze got it or if it's because Ze knew I wasn't hanging up until I'd won. I'm good either way. I fake shadowbox. Quick extend two fists forward with two fingers pointing outward, shouting out to the Wonder Woman. Stretch the back; it is chuff time for me!

Which I thought would be rapidly followed by sleep time, but guess what? I thought wrong.

"You awake?"

It's Imani. It's two thirty in the morning. And yes, of course I'm still awake. I had coding to do. Six hours of it, my crossed eyeballs tell me. I ping back.

"My Dad said we should talk to the people at the New York African Burial Ground."

I google.

The African Burial Ground National Monument is a monument at Duane Street and African Burial Ground Way in the Civic Center section of Lower Manhattan, New York City. Its main building is the Ted Weiss Federal Building at 290 Broadway.

So, they would, I think, be all over this. And maybe they know stuff we don't know, although maybe not yet anyway.

The site contains remains of more than 419 Africans buried during the late 17th and 18th centuries in a portion of what was the largest colonial-era cemetery for people of African descent, some free, most enslaved. There may have been as many as 10,000–20,000 burials in what was called the "Negroes Burial Ground" in the 1700s.

Some free. Most enslaved. I force myself to blink, text a response. "Okay. Adding a page in the app for them. Need to find out who we talk to. Maybe we can rule out burial ground like we have Seneca Village."

"'k." With that, Imani signs off, but I keep reading page after page.

The discovery highlighted the forgotten history of enslaved Africans in colonial and federal New York City, who were integral to its development. By the American Revolutionary War, they constituted nearly a quarter of the population in the city.

New York had the second-largest number of enslaved Africans in the nation after Charleston, South Carolina.

I keep reading that line over and over and over again. *A quarter of the population. The second-largest number of enslaved Africans.* In my city. And somehow I know nothing about it. Which doesn't seem possible. I mean I know all about slavery and the Civil War and Robert E. Lee and Ulysses S. Grant. And Jim Crow. And carpetbaggers.

How can I know virtually nothing about slaves in New York City? How is that possible?

Maybe that's harsh. I do know there were slaves in the early days of New York. I remember something about men on a ship who came with the Dutch West India Company. But, according to my less-than-steel-trap-brain that was even before New York was New York.

EIGHTEEN

School week finally ends, weekend comes, and we descend on the New York Public Library as soon the doors open.

Now if this were a typical weekend excursion, I would be making my way toward Fifth Avenue, deciding which lion I'd greet today. Is it a day for "Patience" or a day for "Fortitude?" I would then approach the library from the now-deemed appropriate side, say hello, and race my way up the steps.

Today I do believe I would say hi to Fortitude. Not that "Patience" wouldn't be good, just that I'm sensing Fortitude would be better, more on target with our mission, but as I said that would be if this were typical.

But today is not typical. Today there will be no hellos to lions.

Instead, today I texted everyone to meet at the New York Public Library on Malcolm X Boulevard in Harlem, where we shall have an extravaganza at the Schomburg Center for Research in Black Culture. It has no lions. I am, however, fervently praying it has a huge light bulb, miraculously shining on a heretofore unknown document, giving us all the answers we need.

In my fantasy world we find a window to sit under, and the crepuscular rays, more colloquially known as Jesus rays, come down and light our way. I'd prefer a musical accompaniment so we know to pay attention before the fickle finger of fate moves along, before that one shaft of light shining on that one piece of paper we need to tell this story is covered by a passing cloud.

Hey, it's as good a needle in a haystack as the rest of my thinking.

Which is pretty all over the map. I twinge at that. But before I meditate on that twinge, from my vantage point down the block I spot Vik and Joe at the entrance caught up in a round of hacky sack, which immediately interferes with my process.

Because I, of course, deliberately left early so I would get here twenty minutes ahead of opening. Which, quick glance at my phone, I have done. And I'm actually the third to be arriving.

And even as I'm heading up the block, not only do I now see Imani and Jimmy rounding a corner, but they're with, I squint, Marcus Johnston, and they're closer than I am. Which will make me fifth to arrive.

I am never fifth to arrive.

"Hey, guys," Imani yells out as she nears. "Marcus and I were talking at rehearsals, and he wants to help out, too."

Or worse, sixth.

Marcus, yes, robotics cocaptain, now costarring with Imani in the musical, and he of the bounciest, silkiest afro ever. He smiles over in my direction, and I don't need to see Imani to know she is smiling before what's coming next even happens, even though we all know it will happen. Yes, I melt. Yes, I know. But it's not like I'm melting because I want to be his girlfriend or something. I'm not interested in dating him. I was, for the record, interested in dating his ex-girlfriend, but that, alas, was a complete nonstarter.

Imani and I have discussed my Marcus reaction, and we think I melt because I just want to *be* him. To melt my way inside, so I can be so chill, so charming, and so pretty that all the girls would want to run their hands through my short crop the way everyone wants to play with his wide, loose, natural fro.

You know, and this is occurring to me just right now, I think I melt because I exist on some level to be Marcus Johnston's pathetic twinabe.

So yes, he's in. Or he will be, as soon as the doors open. Which is really great, since we can def use more thinking, because I have lots of thinking, and sadly not only is none of it great, but worse, none of it's easy.

And none of it feels like a winner.

I take advantage of our momentary delay and sign to Joe, "Is everything okay?" I motion around, meaning with all of us.

He shrugs and grins, signing back, "She'll get over it."

We head downstairs to the Jean Blackwell Hutson Research and Reference area, where there's a small room that allows quiet talking. After everyone downloads the app-in-progress, I begin to lay out the few thoughts I do have.

"We don't have anything concrete at this point, but I did call Tsarnowsky and he promised to follow up on the tests for us. The big thing is the year, which we don't know, but we know its nonconfirmed estimate is roughly somewhere around 1800. So, let's say we have twenty years on either side?"

I look at everyone looking at me, and my face lands in my palm and I smush the right side up and down, pushing my glasses right across my nose, rubbing my now-exposed one eye. There's an overwhelming-ness to all this.

Okay, I start with things I uploaded last night.

"In the app, I flagged a couple of places. I marked the African Burial Ground, but that's an entire topic for us, and I think we need to break down those findings separately."

I wait to see if anyone disagrees, but that's more for me than them. I'm still trying to keep myself out of jackass-friend category again.

"And there was a," my hand extends with one of those 'iffy' gestures, "maybe," I stress, "slave revolt in 1741. I say maybe because they called it that, but it's one of those things like the Salem Witch Trial where they got this one poor woman to testify and, in the end, without any evidence over 100 people were hanged, exiled, or burned at the stake, near the Poor House at the north end of the city and its boundary of Chambers Street. So it might not have happened, but I made it the first flag out of respect, but not for a clue. Because I think if we go with the 1800 estimate it's way too far back, and so anything earlier is ridiculously out."

I pause. Everyone's kind of nodding, but this time I'm not sure if that's in agreement, or just overwhelm-ment.

"I was originally thinking, maybe twenty years on either side, but I'm not sure that's enough. Maybe we need to look at twenty-five? Thirty?"

And all of a sudden, all that reading coalesces into a thought.

"Wait," and I flip through my phone for notes. "I've got it."

And unfortunately the three people who have now come in the room, which they apparently reserved, are not interested. We gather our things, give little apologetic looks, and head back upstairs, eventually landing in the Langston Hughes Lobby, where one, benches are available, and two, talking is allowed.

I now return to my genius thought, which has had the benefit of percolating time.

"In 1799 New York passed a Gradual Emancipation act. It freed slave children born after July 4, 1799, but indentured them until they were young adults. Then, in 1817 they passed a new law, which would free slaves born before 1799 but not until 1827."

My genius does not seem to be resonating. Nobody says anything.

"Okay, yes, it's random. But we have to start searching somewhere and it doesn't make any sense to go back to

124

events that are unlikely, or forward for that matter. So, if it was after 1827, the shackles make less sense."

I blanch. And I shrink down into the bench. And I'm not the only one.

Shackles. Shackles should not make more sense or less sense. Shackles should never roll off one's tongue.

Did you know courage is the root word for encouragement? One you have, the other you give.

Imani is sitting, patiently waiting for me. She nods ever so slightly, an encouragement. She gives. I receive.

I stand up, wiping my now sweaty hands on my jeans, assuming a sense of command and positivity. It's fake, but it will have to do.

"I think we should start by dividing and conquering. I put together a list of resources so we have places to begin."

Punt one.

"Ari, Vik, Marcus, I'm giving you the Slave Voyages and The Trans-Atlantic Slave Trade Database. They're online. It's a collection that tracked slave ship voyages, and where they could they put in names, countries of origin, etc. I will warn you, it's pretty massive. They even have an African Names Database with details of over ninety thousand Africans from captured slave ships or trading sites."

There is fairly stunned and confused silence, which is broken by Vik, still shaking his head. "So, what, your thinking is that we look at hundreds of voyages to see if someone left a note saying, hey find me when you can?"

I wish someone had taken a picture of their faces. I have to say laughing feels good. But not appreciated by those I am laughing at. I smack my cheeks in an effort to no longer be grinning.

"Okay, I know, sounds ridiculous. And it probably is. But my thinking actually is *if* we concentrate on our girl, and we input only those young girls who came to the US, priority for those that came to New York, within our range, maybe we can get to a decently short list, which maybe, I don't know, eventually will cross reference to something that's somehow meaningful."

I don't quite finish with all the razzamatazz I heard when I first thought this up.

Punt two.

"Imani, Jimmy, and Joe, you get the manuscripts, archive, and rare books divisions, where you will be delving into The . . ." I pause to check my notes. "The Lapidus Center for the Historical Analysis of Transatlantic Slavery, where you will find hundreds of rare books and papers, including," I scroll through my notes to read the last part. "Something called the Middleton 'Spike' Harris papers, 1929-1977. There's," back to my notes. "18.2 Linear Feet of it, whatever that means, and at least part of it is a slavery and abolitionist collection."

I look up. Imani is nodding and scribbling.

"Maybe the curators will have some other thoughts once we're digging. There's lots of family collections. I just couldn't tell which ones seemed the most promising."

And cue noise. My two recruits, Jean and his idiot pal, Aaron, come racing in. Just in time for Punt, Rule of Three.

"You two," I point in their general vicinity, so Jean will know I am annoyed. "You get online and pour through the old issues of the *New York Evening Post.* You are to hunt for any article, any advertisement, any anything indicating eight slaves specifically."

"Nope." Marcus interjects. His voice edgy, rough. "We don't know they were slaves. They could have been eight free black people."

I think on that and nod.

"He's right. However, because they were once shackled together, we're going to assume they are some kind of group. So you're looking for anything that indicates a group of at least eight. Missing. Or maybe even found dead. I mean, maybe we aren't even the first to find them. Somebody dug them up, put them back? And you need to go from 1775 to 1830, just to be safe."

"Which reminds me," I hold up a finger, go back to my notes, and then turn back toward Jean and Aaron, "in 1827 there was a paper called *Freedom's Journal*. It was a weekly, and it was the first paper owned and operated by free black Americans. So there's only a couple of years' worth for our timeline at this point. Long shot, but isn't all of it?"

"Question." Marcus leans forward, tightening the distance between us. "What if they aren't from New York? What if they were escaped southern slaves? Then they could have been rounded up long after New York passed this act?"

His questions are rapid-fire, challenging, laced with emotion. And it's hard because he's completely right. Anything is possible. I exhale loudly.

"Look, for right now, everyone's right and it's kind of endless. I mean, hell, maybe they met a whacked-out preacher, chained themselves together, and walked into a pit. Did one of those cult-gone-wild kinds of thing."

I look at Marcus. His jaw is rigid, his stare intense. I look at each of us.

"All we really know today, right now, is we have eight bodies and a range of dates. So, all we can do is build a big grid, and with every piece of information look to rule something out until the closer we get, hopefully gets us to," I exhale, run my fingers through my hair, look back to Marcus. A confession between us. "Honestly? Being lucky."

And I leave it out there, hanging.

Marcus takes it in, nods, and leans back, maybe not all the way, but enough.

"Which reminds me, speaking of lucky, there won't be any luck coming from my thought about the census. I did some more digging," I pick my phone up from the table and scroll, because one, it's easier to read this and get it right, and two, it's easier to read this and not have to watch everyone's reaction.

"It turns out slaves were counted on all federal census records from 1790 to 1840, but they were just a number under the owner. In 1850 and 1860 they actually did include a breakdown but it was only by sex, specific age, and color. 1870 is the first census in which all people, including slaves, were named."

I pause for just a second, click my screen off. "And since that's outside our window, it's of no use."

NINETEEN

And wouldn't this be an amazing story if I told you we went right to the microfilm and there it was, all these years later, just waiting for us to scroll right down and find it. Kind of like that moment in *Ready Player One* when the key is his.

Yeah, not so much.

Not even close. We all work for hours on end, but when you don't know what you're looking for, you're mostly spinning wheels, like a group of mice caged and running in endless circles. A group of mice, which, by the way, is called a mischief, a little something that might be cool were it not so patently false. Mischief we are not.

We are angry. Then depressed. Then sad, morose, angry again, and ultimately glazed over. There is a weight to not knowing. But there is even more weight to knowing we are their only chance.

So we keep at it. All weekend long.

And on Monday we actually get a break. Tsarno texts, tells us to come by around four.

We all manage to get here, including Joe, and we cram into Tsarno's room, where we find yet another person we don't know. Tsarno makes the introduction. Dr. Stephon Black.

He's maybe in his thirties, really close-cropped hair, wearing super hip glasses, a very well-cut suit, can't tell in this light if it's black or really dark navy, with a gorgeous lavender tie and matching pocket square, all of which is offset by his very expensive shoes. This would be one seriously good-looking man if everything about him wasn't so obviously wrapped up in a really tight bow.

It's a weird thing how you can just see some people and it's like the air around them is circling furiously, buzzing with 'don't touch me.' So no big surprise when he turns out to not be a pleasantry kind of guy.

But Tsarno is unfazed, taking his time, finishing the introductions of all of us.

Now since I had the questionably good fortune to be first on and off this receiving-huddle, I'm standing off to the side, watching everyone else come through. Can we say dismissive?

Dude is so antagonistically arrogant that when likes-to-smile, good-natured Joe is introduced, for the first time since I've known him he shockingly code-switches. He suddenly turns one hundred percent mute, no longer using his voice, speaking only in sign.

Then I realize we're all doing it. We're all code-switching, changing formalities, using "Doctor" and not our usual Stephon, and other safe distancing tricks, some linguistic and some physical. Jimmy's suddenly standing in his super tall mode, Vik's opting for deferential, and even Imani as she's shaking hands and saying hello is using her very proper accent, the one I haven't heard since maybe the eighth grade.

Me, I grab a seat and make a conscious effort not to knee bounce. Instead, I keep pushing my glasses back on my nose. I bend over and grab an eyeglass wipe out of my bag, nearly missing Dr. Stephon Black's beginning. Fortunately or not, he is now eyeing me and waits just an extra beat.

Is it possible to both sit up and slouch down at exactly the same time?

"I'm here because Detective Tsarnowsky tells me you plan to find who was in that grave."

Nice intro. Good stress on the "you." Could *you* maybe

keep the sneer of disbelief to yourself? Part of me wants to actually jump up and answer, "no that's not it. You're here because you have a parking ticket you want fixed or something."

"So," Black-the-Disbeliever as I now think of him continues, "he *asked* me to be here and confirm we did find an artifact at the burial site. It was not in the grave but nearby, most likely scattered by hordes of trampling snowballers, which is why it was missed in the original collection."

He takes another break while he glances down at us, the lowly minions gathered below.

I'd like to point out what I think is the obvious. Without the, ahem, trampling snowballers, or at least one trampling snowballer, there might not have been a body, never mind an artifact, but I'm thinking that's an unwinnable.

"Given that the only body which had broken the surface and then been touched was the young girl, and these appear to be remnants from a strand of waist beads, the consensus is they most likely belonged to her. But we have no way of knowing this with absolute certainty."

Okay. Good. I guess.

Apparently, he is finished momentarily, and his arrogant self is just standing here, waiting. So, I'm guessing he thinks he's shared some spectacular tidbit, but I'm not so sure we think so. Aw heck, I go for it.

"What about DNA? Have the results come back?"

The Doc's nostrils flare and I watch him choke back something, so when he answers his disdainful, snotty voice is now laced with repugnance. And although I would not have classified him as warm and fuzzy before, now he's nearly, clearly disgusted. Imani's hand grabs my arm as we all shrink back.

And although he's staring hard, I risk a glance over at Tsarno, who's positioned himself to stand behind the Dr.'s line of sight, leaning casually against the back wall. He gives me a small smile and a shrug. Great.

"DNA is not a magic answer. And it's not going to be one any time soon. When you're sitting at home, watching your TV crime shows, all you see are winners of DNA searches, but they don't show you the losers."

Lots of wide eyeballs, but no one's saying a word. No one.

"For example," Dr. Black continues, calming, I'm guessing, from our lack of saying anything at all. "DNA tells you there is an eighty percent probability that you are descended from people with no earlobes. But that's an eighty percent probability of the sample group they have to work with, a sample group that might be fifty people. On a planet filled with billions."

Okay. I hate to admit this, but his moment here might be totally warranted. I can honestly say I never thought about it this way. I'm totally in the "hey, we've got DNA, let's go solve this crime" camp. I am completely guilty as charged. We can just color me gullible. Bought into the entire DNA solves everything riff.

I wonder if gullible and guilty come from the same word. If they don't, they should.

"In addition." Dr. Black stops talking.

Yeah, that pause is for me again. Apparently, I forgot to put on my listening-even-when-I'm-not face, and the great and wonderful Black-the-Disbeliever is not interested in my inner musings. Bet he'd hate my digressions. I blink, straighten up in my chair, and manage not to snicker as I feel my leg being nudged. I don't need to look, I know it's Jimmy at work.

"We are faced with challenges, particularly the challenge of an inadequate database on contemporary, never mind archaic, African genetic diversity."

And on he drones. I'm sure it's all incredibly brilliant, just not incredibly engaging.

He takes a brief break, reaching behind for a set of papers. As he passes them to us, he returns to his lecture.

Of course, there are only three copies, so we're sharing, and I am scanning as fast as I can while trying to catch some of what he says.

"Teeth, my specialty, are particularly unique carriers of information. The pattern of enamel and dentin formation is clearly demarcated, and it's ringlike, similar in the way you learned about the rings of trees giving us their age."

Teeth? Again with the teeth. First Lolo. Now him.

I read a subhead: "Artificial prognathism with facially flared maxillary central incisors."

Means nothing to me. But the accompanying black and white sketch shows that maxillary prognathism looks like a jutting upper jaw. Not exactly like buck teeth—it's like the whole jaw is set too far forward.

Which, I continue to read, can be an indicator of where someone comes from, "a prognathism with facially flared maxillary central incisors is indicative of West Africa."

Which should be a milestone moment for us, but Dr. Black is back to his platform of pontification.

A tidbit here, a nugget there. Until finally, with a nod to Detective Tsarnowsky, Dr. Stephon Black deems us enlightened enough, finishes,and takes his leave.

As soon as the door shut behind him, seven bodies wheel around, fixing seven sets of eyes on Tsarnowsky, demanding to know "How do you even know him?"

He laughs, rather heartily, I might add.

"I don't. Vonnie does. She's not happy the department can't do more, won't do more. Like you, it doesn't sit right. So, when I saw her and told her I needed a copy of the DNA results because you all weren't giving up, she sent us the very illustrious Doctor Black. I think he's her cousin."

Tsarno shrugs. "When he got here earlier, I tried my best. I did point out to him that telling you whatever he knows might help, but it isn't going to hurt anything. But, you know, come to think of it, he did look pretty pained about it."

And now, forget laughing, Tsarno's nearly hysterical. "But not as pained as you."

He's probably right. We aren't exactly floating on air for people who just got a puzzle piece. I think that man exhausted us.

But, whoever she is, she is West African. And that's something. At least we think. Probably. Statistically speaking.

OMG. We so need food.

And we have to drop Imani and Marcus at rehearsal, so it's too tight for a sit-down anywhere. Ahead, however, there waits an oasis. A falafel truck sits parked, open for business with no wait line and amazing aromas emanating.

Beeline are we.

Our hover while the falafels are being made is broken by Marcus, who crosses the sidewalk, jumps on top of a short ledge, and suddenly begins reenacting the key moment, with a dead-on impersonation and lots of linguistic liberty and improvisation.

"So, my lesser intelligent people, if you are going to get answers, most likely they will not come from a miraculous DNA result. God will not chisel them onto a tablet for you to read."

And while we're all laughing, a crowd is gathering, and some passerby yells out, "Preach!" Which makes everyone louder. Marcus raises his voice by, I don't know, a mere ten times, rising to the challenge.

He calls out to his sidewalk congregants, "No, my lesser beings, they will most likely be delivered unto you from the practitioners of the great and powerful science known as bioarchaeology, or the ancient study of what you might call . . ." Dr. Marcus as Dr. Black mimes reaching back, grabbing a small stack of papers, and passing them about while finishing his sentence with "dem bones."

His right foot taps a count, one two three four.

Your toe bone connected to your foot bone

Your foot bone connected to your anklebone

I start to sign for Joe, but he waves me off, and begins signing with the song as Marcus lifts up his voice and lets go. He is a spiritual master with a street corner pulpit, timing to spare, and rhythm to share.

Your anklebone connected to your leg bone
Your leg bone connected to your knee bone
Your knee bone connected to your thigh bone
Your thigh bone connected to your hip bone

He is clapping low, playing with the still-growing crowd, as charismatic as I've ever seen him, and that's saying something.

Your hip bone connected to your backbone
Your backbone connected to your shoulder bone
Your shoulder bone connected to your neck bone
Your neck bone connected to your head bone

He spins. On toes, freeze. Look up to the sky. Back to the crowd.

I hear the word of the Lord!

He finishes with a big "hallelujah" flourish.

Imani has hold of my arm, my free hand reaches over and grabs for Ari, and we are shrieking and screaming. Over to our right, a small crowd had gathered to watch the display and joins in with their applause before moving along.

One lady walks up, handing him a dollar. As he waves to decline, she grabs his hand and tucks the bill inside, leaving him with a "bless you."

Flashing a cocky smile to go with his new riches, Marcus grabs his falafel from Vikram, his faithful, laughing, head-shaking falafel custodian, and we set off. But the mania that propelled Marcus onto the ledge hasn't burnt itself off, and as we arrive at the school entrance he wheels around, but this time he's not dancing.

He's, I think, bristling, as though his body is pulled taut and then electrified, and he's staring from face to face with an intensity I don't know how to describe. It's as though he's looking at us, but we aren't there.

When he finally speaks, his gorgeous tenor of earlier is gone. He's hoarse, choking, visceral. Seething.

"When?" It's not a question; it's a demand. "Tell me when the fuck it becomes okay to wake up, steal a person, and make them your slave?"

TWENTY

I come up from the subway, making my way home with Marcus's words echoing in my head. It wasn't until he said them that I realized the imitation, the performance, all of it, was rage induced.

And we were all laughing. But then we were all crying. Even big, strong, Jimmy. At least we have each other.

And family. I get home, and everyone's hanging in the living room, waiting for the latest. Since I did drag Jean into helping and then stuck him in the stacks, I do kind of owe him. So I don't bother trying to escape to my room. I join them, bringing them up to speed, trying to summarize the meeting and gloss over the emotions, sticking with the facts as it were, but it's hard, really hard.

Doing it. Hunting for her. Searching through the research, trying to find a thread, even building an app, is incredibly less emotional, less painful than trying to talk about her. The research makes you busy, lets you keep your distance. The words said out loud, as though they are conversational, are all too ugly and too real. Marcus is right. When the fuck does it become okay to wake up in the morning, steal a person, and make them your slave?

"I'm proud of you, Sid."

His voice startles me, and I realize I must have stopped talking. I look at Dad uncertainly. I'm not sure what part of my update would inspire that response. I'm not even sure where I left off. Either way, it's not like I came home with some kind of big news proclaiming we have a name or even a country.

He keeps his voice gentle, his smile loving. "It's very painful to walk through horror you can't understand, torture you can't change, suffering you can't fix, all in an effort to give dignity, to bring peace, and ultimately to bear witness to one person, one *stranger*, all so that their life matters. I'm proud of you. I'm proud of your friends. I'm proud of your brother."

And then I'm somehow off the couch, wrapped up in his arms, being held, and feeling little and big and lost and found and safe and loved. And then we sit, all quietly nestled and chatting, and as I head off to my room I'm feeling calm and connected and that somehow it's going to be okay.

Which, life being what it is, is a somewhat fleeting feeling.

But first, for just a moment, it's pretty great. That savage beast, better known as my brain, is totally soothed and quiet. I'm sailing through updating the app, adding links, compiling info and now, more or less caught up, with a deep breath I'm on my laptop and turning my attention to the *New York Slavery Records Index*, which, according to its home page, has over 38,000 records of individual enslaved people and their owners beginning in 1525, and going all the way through the Civil War era.

Yeppers. So as one might posit correctly, this is precisely why none of us have been rushing to dive in. But now I'm feeling positively bullish. I'm thinking that the year 1800 and West African gives us not much, but a little something to begin any kind of meaningful dialogue with their database.

I'm typing the URL. And it's loading.

And we all knew noiseless brain would not last. What we didn't know was how fast it would blow up, and what would set it off. Turns out, noiseless brain killer would be the words now appearing on my screen, 'The John Jay College of Criminal Justice.'

C'est ouf, ça! It's cray, I know.

Why? Because I've been so overwhelmed I really haven't thought about Ava. Not like I haven't thought about her because I forgot about her, trust me, I don't mean that. I just haven't had time to *feel* about her.

But here is the page, giving whole new meaning to the phrase "fully loaded," John Jay College, home of our first date. Home of the night we first kissed.

What I told Imani is true. I was relieved. I *am* relieved. But being relieved, and knowing she's not good for me, isn't the same thing as not missing her. I truly do miss her. I miss the feeling of giddiness she inspired. I miss the feel of her mouth. I miss the adrenaline rush when she walked in a room. I miss the way I felt when she made want become need. And I miss how she made me laugh.

I look at the screen. I think I don't want to do this anymore tonight. So I won't. I close the computer, turn off the lights, and go to bed.

And I'm dreaming about I don't know what when I hear Jimmy's voice in my dreams saying, "Emergency. Emergency." Only I realize it's not in my dreams, it's in my bedroom, and he's using the computer communication system we built for, well, emergencies when we were kids. It's been so long, I wouldn't even have given using it a thought.

Translation. This has to be urgent and something he won't just text. I bolt out of bed, pull up our old Caesarian Shift Cipher Encoder and get to work.

Thankfully it's short.

"Outside school. Bring I's old makeup kit. Urgent."

I look at my clock, needing confirmation. Yes, it really is five in the morning. This is bad. Adrenaline is now flying. Stand still. It's an order to myself. Imani's old makeup kit.

Think. I can't remember the last time I saw it. It's been forever since we stashed her makeup here.

I circle quietly, eyeballing the room. Dresser. No. Under bed. I pause, visualizing my stack of *Lumberjanes* and other assorted goodness. No. No makeup. And yes! Got it. Upper closet shelf. On the left.

I grab the bag, stashing it and my laptop into my backpack. I pull on clothes, slide quietly down the hall, and, nearly scream. Jean is standing in the hallway, watching me sneak out.

I look at him, frozen. His call. He looks at me, and then his hands move. I look back and gesture, "what?" He rolls his eyes and moves his hands again.

Merde. Write a note. Leave a note.

I turn left, scribble a note, which I leave on the kitchen table.

Forgot we are meeting early. See you later. XO.

Really? XO?

I stick that note in my mouth and grab another paper.

Forgot we are meeting early. Later.

Better. I extract the one held by my mouth and stash it deep in my pants pocket. I reach for the door, turn back, and Jean's still there. I smile, sign "thank you," and very quietly head out into the dark.

Jimmy and Imani are huddled together around the corner from the school, and, even from down the block in the dark I can see Imani's a wreck.

The short terse version is given to me while I both stare and try not to stare at her eye. I half hear how Marcus went nuts in rehearsal, and then he walked out. Imani went after him, trying to calm him down. He went to push her away and hit her by accident. She's okay, but he started sobbing and ran.

I'm not saying anything because I don't know what exactly to say because while the shiner she's sporting doesn't look horrible, it also doesn't look so good. I silently fish out her bag from my backpack and hand it to her.

As she opens it and begins pulling things out, she continues the saga of last night's rehearsal.

"Andy's playing Sancho. So he's singing and hits the line about following his master. And well," she pauses and looks at me for verification. "You saw Marcus last night. So Andy's singing and Marcus just starts screaming, 'this is bullshit', and 'screw this,' and I'm trying to grab hold of him and walk him back, talk him down, something."

I'm trying to say nothing, but I'm guessing my poker face isn't working, because Imani stops, collects herself, and becomes nearly accusatory. "Look, we were all there. We *all* saw him last night."

I cringe, but she's right.

"All of us." Her voice is steady. "But then, I don't know exactly how, it became," her shoulders shrug, her lack of what exactly to say. Finally she goes with, "too much."

Jimmy's been pacing, saying not a word, ever since I got here and Imani started talking, but it's obvious he's heard the story already because Imani is pleading her case directly with me. I'm gonna go out on a limb here and say given Imani's eye, his clenched jaw, and his matching clenched fists, James Flynn is not feeling overly sympathetic toward Marcus. Not that I exactly blame him. I wouldn't put sympathy at the top of my list either.

Unfortunately, lack of poker face must be rearing its ugly head again.

"Look," Imani is not backing down. "I saw my eye this morning, too. I texted Jimmy and flew out the door before my parents were alive and roaming. Only I didn't grab my makeup bag because I didn't want them to see it missing from the bathroom and, I don't know, suspect something."

Imani takes a breather, opens the compact, and passes it to me where my job, previously established over a number of years, is to hold it steady so she can use the mirror.

Imani has me in her direct sight, and Jimmy has finally stopped pacing. With the sun rising and the sky lightening, she can see him reflected in the compact's mirror. "I am swearing to you both it was a complete accident. Marcus was so angry he was just raging, and I walked right into him, and unfortunately right into his flailing hand. I promise."

We all fall silent.

It takes a couple of minutes, but even working with what has to be some old and imperfect concealer Imani renders the bruising virtually unnoticeable. Something I find kind of amazing, but equally really disturbing.

"Now," Imani stares down me and Jimmy. It's an assessment, followed by an order. "We are not going to argue about this. Jimmy, you are going to go and get Marcus. You are not going to do some stupid shit and go beat him up. You are going to grab him and get his ass back here before school begins. And we, that would be you and me, Sid, are going to find Ms. Bessette and convince her not to have him suspended or something."

TWENTY-ONE

And we do manage that. Miraculously. Imani and I stammered through the story, Jimmy got Marcus pulled together, and Marcus threw himself on Ms. Bessette's mercy, and she got it. Or at least, she let it go.

And if that was a miracle, it was a minor one compared to the major god shot awaiting us.

Jean and Aaron are dutifully still pouring through the *New York Evening Posts* and linking anything that might remotely, obscurely, somehow have a tie to our case.

I'm sitting in the main section of the Schomburg Library, clicking through the newest four links Jean's left me, but find nothing that will help us. However, in the last link, I do find the edge of an article, nearly off the page, about the opening of America's first department store, Lord & Taylor, in 1826. I copy and paste it for Imani, figuring she'll get a kick out of it.

And then, because I can, I head down the rabbit hole for a bit. I start clicking, looking for a random headline from every year since the paper began in 1801. *1805, Yellow Fever Epidemic. 1811, Nearly a Hundred Buildings Burn Down on Chatham Street.*

Chatham Street? Now, I admit I'm not familiar with every street in New York City, but you'd think if one hundred buildings burned down, it might be on a street I'd heard of. So now, I must Google-ate.

Park Row was once known as Chatham Street; it was

143

renamed Park Row in 1886, a reference to the fact that it faces City Hall Park, which is the former New York Common.

And that same year, the Commissioners' Plan of 1811 laid out the original design for the streets of Manhattan above Houston and below 155th, putting in place the rectangular grid . . . There were a few interruptions in the grid for public spaces, such as the Grand Parade between 23rd and 33rd, which was the precursor to Madison Square Park . . .

Where you will not find the home of Madison Square Garden. Once you would have, but not now. Hey, at least we've still got the Flatiron.

Back up. That's it. *But not now* . . . I feel it. It's the missing piece. I don't know how, I don't know why, but I know it is.

Central Park, my gorgeous, beloved, massive urban greenspace, which runs from Fifth Avenue all the way over to Eighth, and from Fifty-Ninth Street up to 110th, was not a part of the plan. No one thought about Central Park until the 1850s.

Which, we all knew. Ish. It's the ish that does it, setting off a bout of leapfrog thinking, beginning with Seneca Village.

Because OMG. That was the whole point of Seneca Village and its fight. They were there first, before there was a Central Park. Our bodies weren't buried in Central Park. There was no park. Our bodies were buried in someone's backyard.

And once I have this thought I know it's right. The way to identify these bodies is to find out who owned the land.

I grab everyone and lay out my thinking. "We need to find a map, or maybe the tax rolls, or something. We keep thinking of them as Central Park Bodies, and that's just not accurate."

So, 1811 gets us the Commissioners' Plan. Which in turn, gets us to John Randel Jr. and his ninety-two "Farm Maps." Both the plan and the maps are conveniently online at the Museum of the City of New York.

And these maps are filled with landowners' names for

properties directly in the way of streets being slotted and lots being taken. It's a pretty ugly picture.

And as Joe keeps nudging along the map line, we finally get to the area now known as Central Park, and I hear Imani gasp. I touch Joe's shoulder to signal him to hold, and we all turn to face Imani, who is looking at Jimmy, who nods, confirming their unspoken exchange.

"Her diary." Imani's voice is shaky. She points at the screen, where the name Bessie Seelman is imprinted on a building lot. "Her diary is in the Lapidus collection. We haven't read it, but her name's on one of the slavery indexes, it's there."

A woman. *Wowzerhole.* Of all things I would not have come up with in like a zillion years is that a woman could own slaves. A woman wouldn't even be allowed to freaking vote for what, another hundred years give or take? So she can't vote, but she can own a person?

And yes, my friends, I can hear you. Caution, Sid, this could, of course, be a leap. But somehow, I know it's not. I know our dead bodies are in her yard, and I know that's not going to be by coincidence.

And I know I'm not alone. So you'd think I'd be sharing how we all jumped up, rushing to get to the archives, but I'm not, because we didn't. It's kind of like we all knew and didn't want to be those stupid people in horror movies who go back in the house.

But we would have to be. I believe the answers are going to be in Bessie Seelman's diary. If we walk away, they'd be lost to forever. And we didn't come all this way for lost to forever to be our answer.

We all sit, each lost in our own thoughts, until one by one we rise up until we are nine strong standing together, and we begin walking—a dead man's drag held down by fear and trepidation, pulling ourselves one qualm-laden step at a time to the archive's desk. Imani fills out the form, requests the diary.

It probably takes close to half an hour to get it, and I don't think anyone speaks that entire time. Her name finally called, Imani goes, gets the book, returns, and very gently opens it to the first, fragile, yellowed page. I'm sitting directly across the table, and after she looks down at the book, Imani looks up at me, tears already falling from her eyes.

For a while she says nothing, turning pages as gently as her shaking hand will allow. After her third attempt to turn the page without tearing it, Joe, who took the seat next to her right arm so he could read along, takes the edge and turns it for them both. After his sixth- or seventh-page turn, Imani stops him and reads an entry aloud, her voice trembling, her body shaking.

"Twas a very trifling rain today. The new gurl didst finally arrive. She will be Martha Three. Twas rather late, which didst interfeer with my supper. In truth I didst not like the look of the man who brought her and told George Two to be shur he took his leave."

Martha Three? George Two?

"Ephraim, I didst receive sad news. Your Cousin John hath passed. I beleeve it twas a short illness which hath induced intense suffering. So, it is indeed a mercy. God will have his soul now. I didst tell Martha One I do not like how Martha Three looks at George Five. This be a Christian house. I will not be having such in my house."

Martha One? George Five? The only thing keeping me from laughing out loud or snorting or reacting is knowing this isn't someone's idea of a bad play, but someone's actual diary of their actual life. Some person who thought you could name people with numbers, like they didn't deserve their own name. As though they were not human enough for that.

How human do you need to be to rate your own name?

"Our long spell of fine weather didst end tonight. I feer tis time for a decision before the ground should harden again."

146

"I have had a shock today, Ephraim. It is now ten years since you have gone home to the Lord. Martha One made your favorite supper to remember. I had to tell her again to speak with Martha Three, she be an uppity one. I willst not tolerate pride and vanity in my house."

Imani turns the page, then another.

"I prayed again today. I believe the Lord wilst show me the way."

And another turn of the page.

This one is different. Imani stops turning, sits staring at the page, saying nothing. Joe has read it, and looks up at the rest of us, his face fully distressed. He goes to move the book away, but Imani puts her hand over his, not allowing it. We wait.

"I have decided. I wilst not set free those men I hath paid good money for. Who are these pepul who hath decided slavery no more. I say fie. I bought my goods with fair money. Are they not mine to dispose of as I see fit? Ay. And none shalt tell me different."

"Today I didst purchase a new dress. And then I burned my new dress. And I did so to remind my bruther that what is mine, is mine."

I hear Ari's sob, as much as she is trying to muffle it in Vik's shirt.

"Ephraim, Martha Three wouldst not be to your liking, for she is of a rebellious spirit. Such as I will not tolerate. I brought all the Martha's together and read them Colossians 22: Bond-servants, obey in everything those who are your earthly masters, not by way of eye-service, as people-pleasers, but with sincerity of heart, fearing the Lord. I feer, my dear, Martha Three will not listen."

Jean is sobbing, and I have wrapped him up in my arms. I don't think he's cried in my arms since he was five, maybe six. I smell his hair. I breathe him. I feel how deeply I love him.

"I am glad to be of years to understand thees choices of men

are not for just and fair reasons, but are of reasons of vanity and superiority. Politiks. The devils hand at work."

"Ephraim, I hast found a man. Tis he and his bruther who will come in two days time."

Imani turns another page. I am no longer breathing.

"Tis done. I fear no retribution, not in this life, nor in the next. For twas a good and Christian deed, for where wouldst they have gone? Who would have looked after them, fed them, cloathed them?"

"My mind returns to Colossians. 'Whatever you do, work heartily, as for the Lord and not for men, knowing that from the Lord you will receive the inheritance as your reward.'"

Imani shakes her head, then stops. Tears stream, unchecked, down her face. She closes the book, pushes it to the center of the table, where it sits. Untouched.

It won't matter how many more pages there are as we have our answer. Her name was Martha Three. Martha-fucking-Three. She died with Marthas One and Two and Georges One, Two, Three, Four, *and* Five because she was worth no more than a dress. She died because if Bessie Seelman couldn't have her, neither would anyone else.

I don't know what we expected. I know it wasn't this.

The PA system tells us the library will be closing in another fifteen minutes. Imani retrieves the book, stands, and walks herself and the diary back to the archives desk.

You know when you read novels and they talk about a group of people looking "stricken." Yeah, I don't think I ever truly understood that until today. We are all of one face, one expression. It is more than wounded. It's as if we are cellularly changed, marred by something we can't comprehend and yet our marrow knows it's true. I look at Marcus and see myself. I see he is beyond rage because what lies beyond rage is beyond comprehension. And I see he is me.

Together we zombie our way out the front door. The dark sky, the cold air, the rush of street traffic is unfathomable.

A horn screams loud and long, a rude reentry. We blink. We have traveled so far and been gone for so long.

And now we stand here, no one knowing what to do or say. Our voices still held captive by the unspeakable. My phone pings the ping I'd know anywhere. Tsarnowsky.

I look at everyone and give a forced chuckle. There is bitter irony in the first words that will pierce tonight's air. "He's got the DNA results."

TWENTY-TWO

I can't tell you who was more shocked, Dr. Lena Lolita Renata de la Cortez a.k.a. Lolo or Doc Black or Vonnie. After we met with Tsarno, he called and got them all to come over. And he was having a very good time pointing out what a little interest could do.

And while one could objectively acknowledge it was kind of like finding a needle in a haystack by tripping and having your hand land on it painfully, we did still need to go out and find the right haystack. I therefore admit, it was kind of fun listening to Tsarno relay what we had done.

But what we had done is the problem. It was amazing. It was great. It didn't, however, resolve what we set out to do.

The DNA results did help, but as we knew they weren't a magic bullet. Between all parties, we now know with a high probability, or in lingo-land, we now have a *genetic affinity*. We can posit she came from Senegal and, if so, was most likely transported from Senegambia.

And, although we didn't know it at the time, Tsarno had kept the New York African Burial Ground in the loop, promising if anything were known, they would be the first to be made aware. So they're now looking to put together an exhibit to tell her story. They're also going to take custody of her DNA. As the pool grows and the science progresses, they promise they will someday try to find her family.

All in all, it's a remarkable story. Everyone says so. Repeatedly. So we should be feeling pretty amazing. We did accomplish on so many levels what no one believed we could do. We did find her, and we did tell her story. But her story has no actual name. Which is what we set out to do—to find her name and say her name. So in that sense we failed. And even three weeks later that's what hurts so much.

Even my High Line is not bringing me my usual sense of security or balance. I make my way over to the Plinth, to visit Simone Leigh's *Brick House*, which is this enormous 16-foot-high bronze of a Black woman's head on a torso that "combines the forms of a skirt and a clay house." The head is just this amazing, powerful presence. She's bold and fierce, with an afro framed by cornrow braids, each of them ending in a cowrie shell.

When they first installed her, I learned *Brick House* comes from the term for a strong Black woman, *one who stands with the strength, endurance, and integrity of a house made of bricks.*

I believe she could be Martha Three. And I breathe her in.

Then I take my hand and touch it to her torso. I'll be back. And I start to hustle, now heading my way toward the High Line's very end, Gansevoort Street. At Sixteenth I stop for just a moment to peer out. There she is, small but perfectly framed, my favorite perspective, Lady Liberty. I smile before hustling on.

And then, destination reached. 74 Wall Street, between Pearl and William Streets. Wall Street. Where the geographic heart of New York's Financial District meets the symbolic home of American capitalism. And where the New York Slave Market operated and thrived. I guess this would make it a part of the city's commodities market. You know, where people buy/sell/trade raw products, like cotton, sugar . . . other people.

I stare at the marker, innocuous enough, almost homogenized. But maybe that's not fair. Maybe a single plaque can't capture the horror of an entire people. And, at the very least, it's here.

As opposed to the old Slave Market itself. There's a condo building where it used to stand, and looking at it I wonder if the people inside ever stop to think about what was there before. Whose blood and sweat runs beneath their building. And something about that thought brings me back to another place and time.

Four years ago our class took a school trip to Washington, DC. We went to visit the Vietnam War Memorial. It was breathtaking and sobering all at once. We walked slowly past each piece of the wall, taking in row after row, name after name, each being honored and remembered, if not by family, by history.

After that we had several museums we could pick to visit. Imani went with me to the Holocaust Museum.

As you enter, each person is given an ID card. And each card has a name. Mine said Helen Katz, born January 2, 1931, Kisvarda, Hungary. And there's a photo. It's old and a little blurry, but I can see she was young and had these really big, dark eyes, and long brown, wavy hair pulled back with a left-side part.

I look at Helen, and I take that card with me through the entire museum, starting with the cattle car/elevator up to the top floor. Then we're crossing under the gates telling me *Arbeit macht frei*. Work makes free.

We begin walking our way back down, past the piles of shoes and the Tower of Faces, always with Helen in my hand and in my head.

When we get to the bottom I learn Yaffa Eliach created the Tower of Faces one photo at a time. She was from a place called Ejszyszki in Poland. There were four thousand Jews in that area before the Nazi's came. Only five hundred survived their initial round of massacres. Only twenty-nine survived the war. And on every floor, as you walk by, the Jews of Ejszyszki are vibrantly remembered by this celebration of their lives.

And Helen? At the end of our day, I learned her fate.

On May 28, 1944, the Katz family was deported from the Kisvarda ghetto where they'd been sent. Helen Katz was killed upon arrival at Auschwitz on May 31, 1944.

Helen Katz was 13 years old. I still know her name. I still have her card. She is not forgotten.

Now I stand here in lower Manhattan, running my fingers over the historical slave market marker, the drawing so at odds with the neighborhood now having risen from it. Taken from a 1716 map by William Burgis, where he'd drawn every building on Manhattan's East River shore, now it looks almost like one of those Americana jigsaw puzzles. You know the very manicured lawns ones with perfect quaint houses and a mountain in the background.

I call Imani.

"I'm so sorry." I'm struggling to keep my emotions in hand. Guilt. Sadness. Desolation. Failure.

"For what?"

"I promised you we would find her and say her name. Martha Three isn't her name."

For a long time, there's no answer, but I can hear her breathing so I know she's still there.

"You know, Sid, I have a question for you. Is she, is Martha Three Aldonza or Dulcinea?"

I'm so surprised, it takes me a minute to process she's talking about the play. Her play. *Man of La Mancha.* Is she Aldonza, the whore, or Dulcinea, the lady? Fortunately, this is rhetorical.

"She's both. And she's neither." Imani's voice is clear, strong. She's already traveled this unknowing for herself. "It's the same for Martha Three. And one day, maybe after the DNA pool is so big, and more data is unearthed, and the sky turns purple and fish fly, we'll know who else she is. But who she is, Sid? We do know that. She is not forgotten."

I think about that, breathing loud enough so Imani will know I'm here.

"Maybe we could just call her Three? Like Eleven in

Stranger Things or Seven of Nine from *Star Trek*. Women with numbers are very cool."

"Oh my god, you are such a freak." Imani is laughing hysterically.

I am. She's right; I am a freak. But not freaky enough to mention that way back in the day, in the original *Star Trek* pilot, Majel Barrett is known only as Number One. Nope. Not gonna bring that one up. Instead, I get my announcer voice on, because, well, because.

"Join us, Friday nights, for DNA, the final frontier."

And after just the slightest pause Imani clicks her "engage button." "Fly with us down the double helix road of discovery, starring Three, as the genome of promise."

Oh. Nice one 'Mani. But I'm ready. "Featuring Georges One, Two, Three, Four, and Five as our intrepid team of Genetic Affenites."

"Love you, Sid."

"Yeah, love you too."

I hang up, turning to head home, when it occurs to me that "Three" and Helen have given me something else. A plan.

I enter Mr. Clifton's class at the last possible second, impeccably dressed to kill. Skinny jeans, white man-tailored shirt untucked, with black-and-white bow tie open and dangling loose from the collar and, yes, my spectators—I am a very lean, maybe not so mean, fighting machine.

Jimmy and Vik, of course, are already there as we take this class together. I glance about as I stride to the front desk, confirming, as I'd asked, that Imani, Ari, and Marcus have also made it.

"Mr. Clifton, I would like to present my quote for the table." And cue the screams.

Now, if anyone needs a refresher, Mr. Clifton teaches an AP class called Morality, Legality, and Life. His final is the same every year. Every student must bring in a sticker and argue for its inclusion on his very heavily decoupaged coffee table. Obviously we are welcome to do this at any time, but we only get one shot.

Needless to say, for someone like me, this is crazy-making. Every song lyric, every quote, every bumper sticker I pass might be the one. So I'm just saying it's possible I may have slightly abused my friends' patience trying to find a sticker or come up with a quote I think will justify my contribution.

Even still, my friends do not need to sit here and cheer quite that enthusiastically. Perhaps a little polite applause would suffice.

I roll my eyes at them. Mr. Clifton motions the floor is mine.

"As some people might be aware," and I glare directly at Jimmy, who is still snickering. And then I do that stupid thing I hate. I stand there, with my head cocked slightly, my jaw pushed forward, and I wait.

"I looked everywhere, all the time." I begin with my confession. "Is this one smart enough? Is this one funny enough? And then I learned something unexpected. It wasn't some sticker that I needed to go find. It was meaning. I needed to go find meaning. So I did. And then I went and made my own sticker. And now I'm ready."

Part of me wants to stand here and make everyone wait for it. Anticipation and all that, but I know it's not the kind of thing I can tease. I keep going.

"The quote I've chosen begins with, '*To forget would be not only dangerous but offensive.*' It's the first half of a sentence written by Elie Wiesel, and it's from his book, *Night*. My sticker is actually the second half of his sentence, '*To forget the dead would be akin to killing them a second time.*'"

And that's it. I stand here waiting, not sure what I do next.

The room is now completely quiet. Mr. Clifton sits at this desk, his elbows on the tabletop, his chin perched on his clasped fists, assessing me. I wait, not nervously but maybe a bit uncomfortably. I don't like having to stand here with the "all eyes upon me," but I am confident in my choice, prepared and ready to fight for it. Until then I tell myself over and over "don't fidget."

Mr. Clifton smiles slowly. He nods approvingly and says, "Pick a place." Just like that. No argument needed. So I do. And until it gets covered over, it will remain about two inches from an end, wrapping upward on an angle.

And maybe that's the ultimate irony. It will be there until it gets covered over. And then perhaps it will be forgotten. I never thought about that.

TWENTY-THREE

But after all these weeks, well really months, two and half if you were counting, it is time to breathe again, at least for me. Imani and Marcus are in their final throes of rehearsal.

And four nights later, Jimmy, Ari, Vik, and yes, Joe and I, sit right up-front waiting for the curtain to open and their night to begin.

Somewhere in the back one might find the pack of parents if one were looking, which we are not.

I glance over and watch Joe talking about something with Ari and I realize how happy I am we somehow got joint custody of him. He fits. And houselights to half, so focusing on my assignment I surreptitiously try to get Ze on the line, but sadly not happening.

And now it's too late. House out, light cue one, and enter stage left Marcus as Don Miguel de Cervantes.

The applause is thunderous. And as he delivers his opening monologue, he turns, walking downstage, until he is upon us.

And as he is telling us of Don Miguel de Cervantes' intention to go out in the world as a knight-errant, I take one last time to look at Marcus, to think of our adventures, and then, then I sit back and let the music, the moment, the rightness of it all wash over me.

When it's over, we head backstage for a group hug that means so much more than we ever knew it could. And with that it's cast party time.

And here, my friends, is when I shall omit a few details. You might recall discretion, the saying goes, is the better part of valor. Suffice it to say, it involved fake IDs, a piano player, and a room filled with imbibers of the drunk, drunker, and drunkest kind, singing show tunes loud, proud, and pretty well on key. A good time was had by most is a fair summary.

Imani and I somehow get back to her place somewhere around two.

We are, to stay in our moment, fairly well debauched, or, in more modern lexicon-ology if you prefer, pretty well lit. I am so musically funny when, let's just say, pretty well lit. We're definitely somewhere on the very happy scale, stumbling about, and loudly shushing each other. Miraculously neither of her parents put in an appearance. I think we can safely guess this is a choice. There're only so many times you can sneak in and say "shhhhh" before you wake them.

As a matter of fact, because I've slept over so many times and this isn't our first attempt at sneaking in, the number of times it actually works is less than once, also known as never.

So tonight, or this morning, they are graciously ignoring us, and we are having a sleepover. I don't think I've slept over in, wow it's got to be at least over a year.

Imani's gone back out to the kitchen, and I'm propped up on her bed, just taking in old, familiar surroundings. There are so many pictures of us. I smile. There's one with Ze. Oh wow, there's even one with Tsarnowsky in it. And there are a bunch of new ones of just 'Mani and Jimmy.

Small pang.

Oh, not about the two of them. They're such old news I don't even think about it anymore. No, it's a small pang for Ava. But just a small one.

Imani comes back, carrying a huge bucket of freshly popped, or at least freshly microwaved, popcorn. Which, once I get a whiff, all protest thoughts of not being hungry fly directly out the window. Instant stomach growl.

She plops down on her side of the bed and my hand snakes right on over. "I can't remember the last time we did this."

Imani laughs, "Me neither."

She passes me the bowl and reaches over to grab the remote.

"And, wait for it, it gets even better. I did some research and found us something to binge."

Oh my god, it really has been forever since we did this. We used to prop up Imani's laptop between us, share one set of headphones, and stream something, sometimes really anything, all night long. Hours of stupid cat videos on our way to making it through, I think sixty-two, of some list's top movies ever made. We sang through musicals, including one night where we watched *Grease* four times in a row before we passed out.

We also watched every lesbian show ever made I think. We even watched pieces of shows if they had a snippet of lesbian or sometimes just the aroma of lesbian. All a show needed was l-attitude a.k.a. lesbian attitude, and you got a viewing slot.

OMG, I laugh to myself. I remember the day I found out Rizzo was in a lesbian movie. *The Truth about Jane.* Yes, I know Stockard Channing isn't Jane, but I don't care. She's Stockard Effing Channing and she rules. We got a copy and watched it that very weekend.

But I'm A Cheerleader, Saving Face, Desert Hearts, and finally, both our favorite, *I Can't Think Straight.*

By the time we found *I Can't Think Straight,* I knew for sure, and so did everyone else. Imani helped me tell my parents, and then Jimmy—not that, come to think of it, it was overly shocking to any of them.

After that, between Imani and Jimmy, it was a floodgate of downloads, a tsunami of titles. Even if someone was just a guest star dying in the background of a show, if they were gay, they went on a list and we watched it. The more obscure, the better. Or if they were even super kick-ass they qualified on both potential and aspirational points. Sigourney Weaver because, well, Ripley; Charlize Theron, a triple threat with Furiosa, *Atomic Blonde*, and *Monster*, and let's not even begin listing the supersheroes.

I want to make a movie with all of them and call it *Butch Like Me*. Or maybe, *Butch Like Me Wanna Be*.

Maybe Samantha Sidley's *I Like Girls* will be the opening credits kind of like Adele's *Skyfall* and Bond. Of course, then I'd have to change my title, which I don't think works for me.

"So, I'm skipping season one." Imani's voice suddenly interrupts my trip down movie memory lane, as she's already cued something up and is hitting the pause button. I have managed to miss the entire event. "It's really not important, and it's already after two in the morning. I will, however, give you the CliffsNotes version, so we can jump right into season two, and you will be just fine."

My eyebrow must have quirked because Imani pauses long enough to blow me off with, "you don't need it; pay attention."

Now, she is all business.

"So, in Season One of *Janet King*, we meet Janet King, played by Marta Dusseldorp. She is a striking blonde lawyer, now heading up some kind of commission. It's an Australian show, so the details aren't exactly the same. In your missing season one, she had this intense case, and in the end the coparent of her twins is murdered. Tony, played by Peter Kowitz, is her loving and exasperated, often funny, charming boss."

Imani comes up for air, but for just a second.

"Anyway, probably too much info. Season Two picks up a couple of years later, Janet King is returning to work with this appointment, she's going to bring in some of her old gang, and here we go."

And with that, Imani poofs her pillows, hits the enter key on her computer and we're watching.

I suppose my logical question would be how does she know I've never seen it. The answer will soon be clear.

Although Imani won't be awake to know it. I don't know exactly when she fell asleep. I don't know because I am spellbound. From pretty much the moment when Anita Hegh shows up as Inspector Bianca Grieve, I am team Bianca.

It's somewhere about six in the morning when I feel Imani move and roll over. With only eight episodes and some incredibly pointed and judicious fast forwarding, I am nearly done.

"Well?"

"It's good."

Imani snorts. "Not that, you dodo. Team Janet or Team Bianca?"

I feel the blush, but it's still dark in the room as I confess, "Bianca."

"Hah. I knew it." Imani's voice is still all groggy. "Jimmy owes me ten bucks."

"Wait." I'm thinking I may have to be appalled. "You bet on this?"

"Oh yeah. When I found this show, he said you'd be all over the blonde. For the record, Vik agreed with me, but Ari went with Jimmy. I said there was no way. Blonde chick is way too mean for you." Imani picks her head off the pillow and grins at me, incredibly lopsidedly. "You don't like mean. You don't have those defenses."

And with that she rolls back over, curling into a ball.

"Hey, 'Mani, why didn't you say anything when I was trying to sort Ava?"

For a moment there's no answer and I wonder if she's going to pretend she's fallen back asleep. But she answers, "Because my job wasn't to tell you what to feel or how to feel. My job was to wait for you to feel and be here when you did."

I think on that for a moment when the immortal words of my newly beloved Bianca flit across my mind, "great things never came from comfort zones."

I sit watching the rise and fall of the blankets as Imani dozes back off, and memories flood through my mind. The first time I slept over, both of us getting ready for bed in our flannel pajamas—hers with unicorns, mine from the boy's department with computer circuitry—suddenly so awkward. Pillow fights. Blanket forts. She was the first girl I kissed. Wow. I'd kind of forgotten about that. No, not forgotten. I just hadn't thought about it in a while, a long while. Wow.

It was a Friday night. I had decided I might be gay, maybe, but I didn't know how I was supposed to know for sure. I can still see Imani, so sincere, so incredibly sweet, telling me I should kiss her, and if it works then we would know.

I surprise myself and laugh aloud at that memory. A small snore is my only answer.

I keep replaying memories until I am no longer awake, just sitting up. Finally, I slide down, deeper into the bed, my head on the pillows, listening to Imani's quiet breathing.

And I smile and roll over. Just like when we were kids.

Me and 'Mani. Besties forever.

Acknowledgments

With each new escapade, my list of gratitude grows, but it always begins with you, my readers. Thank you for embracing Sid, Jimmy, Imani, Vikram, and Ari. To the librarians, bloggers, reviewers, fellow authors, and wonderful friends who continue to support me on this extraordinary journey, I appreciate you, and every kindness you have gifted me.

And if you've read this far, please join me in recognizing, and in saying thank you, to those whose lives were stolen by slavers and sold to build my city, the City of New York, and my country, the United States of America. We may never know their names, but we owe them all a debt of gratitude, an honored place in our history, and a world in which they are always remembered.

As with all of Sid's grand adventures, it takes a small world of "otherly brilliant" people to make it real. Joe Saraceni, I am smiling big while the fingers of my "flat hand" are coming up to my lips, and now moving down and forward, right at you. Thank you. And Ellen Burditt, thank you too, for reading and checking, and reading again.

Dr. Craig O'Connor of the Office of Chief Medical Examiner of New York. I hope I have taken your generously given time and explanations, and delivered them into my story with clarity and accuracy resembling what you gave me. Thank you so very much.

Dr. Michael L. Blakey. First, thank you for all your work on the African Burial Ground project, and then, thank you for your insights on my thinking for this story. You may have altered my direction, but in return, gifted me an especially emotional core.

To the myriad of people who answered cold calls, and graciously shared their time, talent, and expertise to help hone my story, including Michelle Commander, Associate Director and Curator of the Lapidus Center at the Schomburg Center for Research and Black Culture; Sara Cedar Miller, Central Park Conservancy; Dr. Hannes Schroeder, Section for Evolutionary Genomics, The GLOBE Institute, University of Copenhagen; and Sachi Gerbin, The Science & Entertainment Exchange, of the National Academy of Sciences, thank you all for being the most generous of resources.

And Magdalena, thank you for teaching Sid the rules of "expletivities."

For Friends who are Family …

Fay Jacobs, there is never an eleven o'clock number big enough for all your help, first as my friend, and second as my editor. So let's toast instead to *more misadventures!*

Bywater Books. Salem West, Marianne K. Martin. Editors: Elizabeth Andersen, Carleen Spry – come on, what's a few extra commas between friends.

Russell Kolody. Shamim Sarif. Hanan Kattan. Rachel Talalay. Bonnie Quesenberry. Cheryl A. Head. Ann Aptaker. Jesikah Sundin. Amanda

June Haggarty. Tiffany Razzano. Lloyd Segan. Shawn Piller. Pam Kozey. Caroline Stites. Elizabeth Coit. Gregory Murphy. Michael Boyle. Brenda Abell.

And Ann McMan, thank you once again for gifting my words with your incredible art.

For Family who are Friends ...

Bernice. Cara. David. Jake. Andie. Evan. Joan. Hannah. Mike. Maddie. Kathleen. Shannon. Andy. Lori. Mark. Josh. Eric. Sheri. Rudy. Emily. Madison. And Neal.

For now, and forever ... for Nancy Prescott ... with all my love.

About the Author

STEFANI DEOUL is the author of the award-winning novels *The Carousel, On a LARP,* and *Zero Sum Game.* She has written for numerous publications, including *Curve Magazine, Outdoor Delaware* and *Letters from CAMP Rehoboth,* penned short stories, and written both film and television treatments. As a television producer her resume includes TV series such as *Haven* for the SyFy Network, *The Dead Zone, Brave New Girl, Dresden Files* and *Missing.* Follow her at www.stefanideoul.com.

Bywater
BOOKS

At Bywater Books we love good books about lesbians just like you do, and we're committed to bringing the best of contemporary lesbian writing to our avid readers. Our editorial team is dedicated to finding and developing outstanding writers who create books you won't want to put down.

We sponsor the Bywater Prize for Fiction to help with this quest. Each prizewinner receives $1,000 and publication of their novel. We have already discovered amazing writers like Jill Malone, Sally Bellerose, and Hilary Sloin through the Bywater Prize. Which exciting new writer will we find next?

For more information about Bywater Books and the annual Bywater Prize for Fiction, please visit our website.

www.bywaterbooks.com